CW0045B490

Storytelling, practised with full consciousness and an oxygenated sense of responsibility, is one of the most dangerous and liberating of human activities. Life is dangerous. It is not surprising that stories are also sometimes dangerous. A mutant star, red hot in its brief ascendancy, sometimes rules over the fates of true storytellers. But another star, golden in its universal glow, confers great hidden benedictions and blessings on practitioners and readers alike.

Regardless of the ambiguous dark side, artists always feel the craftsman's cool ecstasy and the dreamer's serene joy when creating. And the reader always feels the joy in the dangers when immersing.

BEN OKRI
A Way of Being Free

Château d'Argol

JULIEN GRACQ

Château d'Argol

Translated from the French by
Louise Varèse

PUSHKIN PRESS
LONDON

This edition first published in 1999 by
Pushkin Press
22 Park Walk
London SW10 0AQ

British Library Cataloguing in Publication Data:
A catalogue record for this book is available
from the British Library

ISBN 1 901285 14 6

Set in 10$^1/_2$ on 13$^1/_2$ Baskerville
and printed in France by Expressions, Paris
on Rives Classic Laid

Cover illustration: *Five*
Orsina Sforza

Château d'Argol

I

ARGOL

ALTHOUGH THE COUNTRYSIDE was still hot with all the sun of the afternoon, Albert braved the long road that led to Argol. Taking shelter in the already lengthened shadows of the hawthorns, he started on his way.

He was giving himself one more hour to relish the throes of chance. A month ago he had bought the domain of Argol—its woods, its fields, its dependencies—unseen, on the enthusiastic—or rather mysterious—recommendations (Albert recalled that unwonted guttural accent of the voice that had decided him) of a very dear friend, but a rather more than seemly fanatic of Balzac, of stories of the *chouannerie*, and of Gothic romances as well. And without further deliberation he had signed this mad petition to chance for clemency.

He was the last scion of a rich and noble family, little worldly however, who jealously and long had kept him within the lonely walls of an isolated provincial manor. At the age of fifteen all the gifts of mind and physical beauty were seen to flower in him, but he turned from the triumphs which everyone, with singular assurance, predicted for him in Paris. Already

9

the demon of knowledge had taken possession of all his mental powers. He visited the universities of Europe and preferably the most ancient ones, those in which the masters of the Middle Ages had left traces of a philosophical learning rarely surpassed in modern times. He was seen at Halle, Heidelberg, Padua, Bologna. Everywhere he went he was conspicuous for the extent of his knowledge, the brilliant originality of his views, and, while he made few friends, what was matter for even greater astonishment was his unalterable disdain for women. Not that he fled from them, but without ever deviating from a calm and constantly restrained demeanour, he knew the art, once he had entered into intimate relations with them, of defying them with such abnormal and coldly extravagant challenges that even the bravest in the end would pale, vexed at having displayed what he was quick to stigmatize as fear, and would, although regretfully, leave him to pursue elsewhere his consistently nomadic and nonchalant career. Sometimes an essay, rich in particularly valuable subject-matter, an article testifying to a unique and masterly documentation, would appear delighting and, at the same time, troubling, because of all it revealed of fantasy in the tastes and in the soul of its author, the few loyal friends he still possessed in the Parisian world of letters.

In these last few years the beauty of his countenance, with its ever-increasing pallor, had assumed an almost fatal character. The firm lines of the forehead, formed of two prominent lobes, were lost in the gossamer blond hair, of so tenuous a texture that the wind playing through it would untwine and stretch out each dry, divided curl—an extremely rare phenomenon peculiar to certain physiognomies consecrated to the always wearing pursuit of abstract speculation. The delicate straight nose was made of a velvety, matt substance with mobile and extremely contractile nostrils. In his eyes nature had set an insidious snare: their axes not having been made rigorously parallel, they fascinated by their air of looking *behind* the person at whom he was looking, and seemed to convey, as though physically, the burden of an illimitable inner reverie—and in his sidelong glances, the pure white then showing, would disconcert like the sudden and inhuman sign of a demigod. A peculiar propensity to swelling was noticeable in his full lips.

The set of his neck was graceful, and the broad deep chest seemed made to *sink* emotions *to the bottom*. The long thin fingers of the ardent and unquiet hands appeared endowed each with a separate life and, with every slightest movement, marvellously expressive, graceful and infinitely flexible. Such was this angelic and meditative visage: an air from loftier regions, volatile and keen, wreathed the forehead where light had its abode, but at every instant the spirituality of this countenance was exorcised by the carnal, the mortal elegance of the body and the long well-knit limbs; there, too, snares were set; an importunate elasticity, a slumbering heat, the mysteries and magic of too rich a blood invested his arteries: a woman would have longed to fall helpless into those arms as into a sanctuary, a prison. Such was this magnetic figure qualified to penetrate life's subtlest arcanas, to embrace its most exhilarating realities.

It was especially, as we have seen, toward philosophical studies that his mind first turned. At twenty, abandoning all thoughts of success or a career, he had set himself the task of solving the enigmas both of the sentient world and of the world of thought. He read Kant, Leibnitz, Plato, Descartes, but the natural bent of his mind drew him to the more concrete, the more courageous, as some have dared to affirm, philosophies that, seizing the world bodily, as it were, and generously, and not satisfied with illuminating it with any one particular ray of light, but taking into account all its component parts, exact of it its *total* truth and explanation, like Aristotle, like Plotinus, like Spinoza. But above all his passionate curiosity had been stimulated by that prince of philosophical geniuses, Hegel; for that king of the architecture and the science of *wholes,* for the philosopher who has uncrowned, and divested of its glory, all abstract learning, and for whom the most brilliant philosophical systems are only nebulae out of which he composes his gigantic milky way, he had recently conceived an energetic predilection: he looked upon dialectic as that lever which Archimedes had derisively called for which would enable him to lift the earth, and he took Hegel with him to his lonely manor in Brittany, superabundantly to fill his days which he foresaw dull and arid in a melancholy region.

The wild and desolate character of the country, to which chance had so strangely banished him for several months, was not long in impressing itself upon his mind, now calmed by the monotonous rhythm of his walk. To his right stretched flat moorlands filling the eye with the dull besetting yellow of the gorse. Here and there stagnant water lay in grassy bogs where uneven stones offered the surest footing in the midst of a perfidious soil. Toward the horizon, the land seemed to be raised in a fold of ground forming a low chain which had been carved by erosion into three or four higher pyramids. The declining sun was now painting the short grass of the mountains a magnificent yellow: on their summits, jagged sandstone teeth and rude columns of crumbling stone blocks stood out sharply against the sky; a keen air, a luminous sky,

silvered as though by the reflection of the ocean
close at hand, gave a sort of majesty to the clean-cut
profiles of the mountains. To the left rose dark and
gloomy woods, dominated by oaks with, here and
there, a few gaunt pines; invisible brooks could be
heard, but Albert was struck by the rarity of bird
songs and by their sad monotony.

Not far off, an elevation running parallel to the
road cut off the view on that side; along its crest
parasol pines against the setting sun seemed to
accentuate with their elegant horizontal branches the
outline of the ridge, and for an instant gave to the
landscape the unexpected delicacy of a Japanese
print. The western breeze fiercely tossed the tangled
branches of this sequestered forest, hurtled the great
grey clouds, and man seemed absent from these soli-
tary regions. This sensation of solitude began at
length to weigh on Albert's spirits, so that when,
through an opening in the branches, he glimpsed
and thought to identify by a hitherto unfamiliar
beating of his heart, the towers of the manor of
Argol, he felt a singular sensation of relief and, in
every sense of the word, of recognition.

The castle rose at the extreme end of the rocky spur
Albert had been following. Branching off from the
road at the left, a tortuous path led up to it—*impractica-
ble for any vehicle*. For some distance it serpentined

through a narrow strip of marshland where Albert could hear the plunging of frogs as he passed. Then the path started steeply up the mountainside. The silence of the landscape now became complete. Masses of enormous ferns, shoulder-high, bordered the path; on either side brooks of an amazing limpidity ran silently over their stony beds, and dense woods hugged the path jealously in all its windings up the mountain. During the entire climb the highest tower of the castle, overlooking the gorges up which the traveller painfully made his way, shocked the eye by its almost formless mass composed of brown and grey schist roughly cemented and pierced by rare openings, and ended by engendering a sensation of uneasiness that was almost intolerable. From the top of this mute sentinel of the sylvan solitudes, the eye of a watcher following the traveller's steps could not for an instant lose sight of him throughout all the twisting arabesques of the path, and if hate should be waiting ambushed in this tower, a furtive visitor would run the most imminent danger! The merlons of this powerful round tower, made of granite slabs, were silhouetted always *directly over the head* of the traveller toiling up the path, and rendered even more startling the flight of the heavy grey clouds as they rushed past with ever-increasing velocity.

At the moment Albert reached the summit of this steep ascent, the castle's entire bulk rose abruptly out of the last concealing foliage. It then became apparent that the façade completely barred the narrow tongue of land forming the plateau. Built onto the high round tower on the left, it consisted entirely of a thick wall of blue sandstone set flat in greyish cement. The most striking characteristic of the edifice was the flat roof fashioned into a terrace, a very unusual feature in so rainy a climate. The top of this high façade drew a hard horizontal line across the sky, like the walls of a palace gutted by fire, and because, like the tower, it could only be viewed from the foot of the wall, it produced an indefinable impression of *altitude*.

The form and the disposition of the rare openings were no less striking. All notion of *stories*, so inseparably connected today with the idea of harmonious construction, seemed totally lacking. The few windows cut into the walls were almost all at varying heights suggesting an amazing arrangement within. The low windows were in the form of narrow rectangles, and it was evident that the architect had been inspired by the design of loopholes often cut through the merlons for the firing of culverins. No coloured stones ornamented the borders of these narrow fissures that opened in the naked wall like disquieting vent holes. The high windows, ogival in form, were astonishingly lofty and narrow, and the direction of the long, slim, almost writhing lines stood out in overwhelming contrast to the heavy horizontal top of the granite parapets of the high terrace. The leaded panes of the windows were all of angular and irregular shapes. The low narrow entrance door, made of panels of carved oak studded with shining copper nails, opened at the foot of the watch tower to the left of the façade.

A square tower was built at the right corner of the façade. Less high than the watch tower, its roof of slate was in the form of a slender pyramid. It was striped with long vertical ribs, made of granite blocks roughly joined, that could have served as sufficient footing for an agile climber to clamber to the top. Beyond this tower began the steep slopes of the other side of the mountain that plunged into a second valley where, under the monotonous frothing of the trees, the murmuring of water could be heard. Behind this tower and parallel to the valley was a second wing, forming a regular square with the façade. Built in the Italian style like the palaces Claude Gelée loved to scatter over his landscapes, it made a perfect contrast to the gloomy face of the manor. Here could be seen elegant triangular pediments, balustrades of white stone, and windows of noble proportion that seemed to be illuminating gay apartments within; the plain surfaces of the walls were covered with a light stucco that glittered through the leaves, and at the top of a tall staff two pennons of red and violet silk clacked in the breeze. The narrow tongue of land that lay between the great mass of the castle and the gorges up which the path serpentined, was covered with a short springy grass of a brilliant green that enchanted the eye. It was unmarred by any path: the door of the castle opened directly on to the soft carpet of the greensward, and this curious anomaly, considered in relation to the primitive and difficult character of the approach, did not fail to astonish Albert.

He had hardly taken a step across the grass when one of the servants of the castle came forward silently to meet him. The face of this Breton, whose step on the close-cropped lawn unconsciously took on an air of majesty, seemed stamped with a feral immobility. He bowed respectfully and preceded Albert into the castle.

Albert now perceived that the abnormal disposition of the interior, which the appearance of the façade had suggested to his imagination, was not belied. The visitor first entered a lofty vaulted hall with Romanesque arches, and divided by three rows of pillars. The slanting rays of the sun coming through the low horizontal loopholes seen in the façade, and that the setting sun now lighted with long streaks of dancing golden dust, formed with the white pillars a luminous pattern separating the entire upper part of the vaulted ceiling, and their ever-changing and fantastic fluctuations prevented the eye from measuring its true height. No furniture was to be seen in this hall, but here and there piles of deep furred skins; and cushions, covered with Asiatic silken fabrics of an extravagant luxury, were piled against the naked walls and pillars with an air of negligent profusion, making one think of a night encampment of the Golden Horde in a white Byzantine cathedral. Out of this great entrance hall opened low and endlessly winding corridors interrupted by stairways and steep descents full of recesses and corners, which seemed to run like veins through the vast structure of the castle, presenting the appearance of a three-dimensional labyrinth.

Most of the rooms seemed destined for no definite purpose: tables of ebony, divans of sombre leathers, sumptuous draperies seemed to be distributed without the least idea of order. And what was most astonishing about all the furniture was its air of constant *readiness*. The long, low dining-room was lined with sheets of copper set with quadrilateral crystal mirrors; one massive piece of solid copper formed the table, and against its smooth and shining surface burst the dull red of great tufts of flowers. The yellow beams of the setting sun now shone full on this cuirass of incarnadined metal and called forth rich and potent harmonies: the dull red of the massed flowers appeared almost as blocks of darkness—emblems of a solemn and noble melancholy. But as clouds passed by, cruel flashes glided over the walls, pools of unctuous light, viscous and dubious, fell on the table and on the delicate bezels of the mirrors; and the hard brilliance of the metal, of these hostile walls, forced the soul to take refuge in its own centre and seemed to concentrate all thought in a point of flame, sharp and penetrating as a steel blade. Next, Albert passed into the main drawing-room of the castle and could scarcely suppress an exclamation of surprise. The drawing-room was considerably larger than any of the other rooms of the manor. But its height, in particular, was at least triple: the ceiling was apparently formed by the upper terrace of the castle and the apartment suggested the proportions of a vast covered well perforating the edifice from top to bottom. The furniture of the room, as though crushed by the enormous height, seemed to be squatting on the ground, and consisted of piles of white and grey furs forming low couches, tables of ebony and mother-of-pearl, gracefully carved pieces of Breton oak, deep and low tapestried armchairs loaded with cushions of a sulphuric yellow, so brilliant that a sort of phosphorescence seemed to emanate from it, and which can only be compared with a certain yellow to be seen in some of Gauguin's paintings. Rectangular tapestries of faded hues only partially concealed the white stone walls.

But above all, the unique, the wonder-working effect of the room came from the disposition of the lighting. Through horizontal loopholes surged continuous sheets of light that divided the apartment in height by immaterial pulsating partitions almost entirely concealing the ceiling, which was made of a scaffolding of rough beams and gables through whose interstices the sun, coming through a skylight, fell in long streamers to the floor. The ogival windows, piercing the thick walls, separated the room, in their turn, into clean-cut vertical panels of raw light, leaving zones of rigid shadow between them where the eye came to rest on lustreless surfaces. In the lower portion of the hall, the tall pointed windows were hung with a light silk fabric intricately patterned in leaves and flowers; this filtered light, glaucous and softly yellow, seemed to be coming from some marine depth, and bathed the entire lower regions of the room in a uniformly warm glow like a luminous sediment, transparent and compact, while a few feet above, throughout the entire upper plane, the fierce rays of the sun ran riot. This stratification made each plane immediately apparent to the eye, and the contrast between the extravagant luxury displayed in the soft light of the ground level and the rough ceiling where the magic of sunlight in all its power alone held sway overwhelmed the soul with a sort of delirious bliss, warming Albert's heart, as he started up the turret stairs of varnished wood that creaked with every step and were as sonorous as a ship's hull.

As he emerged from the stairway out onto the castle terrace like the bridge of a tall ship riding the waves, the full splendour of the sunlight, until now merely *interpreted* by the copper plates, the slender ogives, the thick and silken walls, burst upon him in all its unbridled freedom. The fresh and powerful breeze that swept the terrace and bowed down the ocean of trees two hundred feet below, fairly took his breath away. The dishevelled folds of the silk pennons, that could be heard clacking now close at hand, like a ship's sails, sent dancing shadows flowing everywhere, and the eye was dazzled by the billowing light on the white stones. Meanwhile this feast of sunlight seemed to spread over utterly solitary wastes. Toward the north where the rocky spur ended in abrupt precipices, the high moors, yellow and smooth, were cut by the capricious wanderings of a deep valley filled with trees that appeared to stop abruptly, as though the rude breath of the ocean had sheared off every branch and twig rising above the level surface of the plateau. At a distance that to the eye seemed infinite, the valley, as it spread out, cut the line of cliffs marking the horizon, and through this triangular notch a small bay could be seen edged with foam and bordered by white, deserted beaches. This little inlet, where not a sail was to be seen, startled the eye by its perfect immobility: it looked like a smear of deep blue paint. Beyond this notch, the low chain that Albert had noticed from the road hid the cliffs from view, and here undulating country began, a stark bold landscape without a tree to be seen anywhere. Great greyish marshes extended along the foot of the last slopes as far as the eastern horizon.

To the south stretched the highlands of Storrvan. From the foot of the castle walls the forest spread out in a semicircle as far as the eye could see: a wild and gloomy forest, a sleeping forest whose absolute stillness seemed to clutch the soul. It encircled the castle like the coils of a heavily inert serpent whose mottled skin was almost imitated by the dark patches of cloud-shadow as they ran over its rugose surface. These clouds in the heavens, flat and white, seemed to be floating at an enormous height over the green abyss. And the sight of this green ocean filled one with an obscure disquietude, giving Albert the curious feeling that this forest *must* be alive, and that, like a forest in a fairy tale or in a dream, *it had not yet said its first word*. Toward the west, high rocky barriers covered all over with trees, ran parallel; a brimming river flowed through these deep valleys, its surface roughened by a gust of wind, like skin by the cold, and suddenly

thousands of bright facets reflected the blinding sunlight with a radiance that was curiously immobile. But
the trees remained mute and menacing up to the blue
heights of the horizon.

Albert opened a low door leading into the round
tower that overlooked the terrace. He found it furnished as a study with shelves of precious woods and
with four oval windows from which the eye could view
all the divers landscapes of the countryside around the
castle. In the bed chambers situated in the upper portion of the edifice, that sumptuous prodigality of furs,
so noticeable the moment one entered the castle,
became a sort of haunting leitmotif, reiterated everywhere. They were scattered in profusion on the floor,
while the walls were hidden by fur panels made into a
chequered design of richly worked skins of the snow
leopard and the polar bear, alternating regularly. A
lavish *negligence* seemed to hold sway everywhere; even
the beds appeared to consist simply of a heap of furs.
The long low anomalous openings, which Albert had
noticed in the façade, were here made use of to pro-
cure a particular effect: each room was lighted by
these long horizontal apertures only three feet high
and not more than one foot from the floor, extending the whole length of the wall against which the
bed was placed, so that on waking the sleeper was
forced to plunge his eyes into the abyss of trees

below, and might fancy himself wafted on a magic ship over the deep billows of the forest. In the corner of the room opposite the bed, a basin of light-coloured marble was sunk in the floor, and toilet accessories, shining with the clean brightness of surgical instruments, offered a pleasing contrast to the long silky whiteness of the furs.

The library occupied the top of the square tower. Wooden panels carved with scenes from *Works and Days* ran all around the walls, but without extending to the ceiling they left a large frieze of dull white stone visible above them, and this refuge of thought was lighted by panes of thick green glass, symbols of the all-powerful and living hope of knowledge, and was furnished with lecterns of carved oak. Albert lingered there, fingering the pages of many of the curious ancient volumes with iron clasps, but a noise as of leaden grains pelting against the window-panes made him look up; the rain was beating on them violently, and anxious to witness the alteration of the landscape the elements now offered, he hastened to make his way to the terrace again.

The storm was raging over Storrvan. Heavy clouds with jagged edges rushed out of the west, almost brushing against the tower, and at moments enveloping it in streamers of vertiginous white mist. But the wind, above all the *wind* filled space with its unbridled and appalling power. Night had almost fallen. The tempest, passing as though through a head of fragile hair, opened quick fugitive furrows through the masses of grey trees, parting them like blades of grass, and for the space of a second one could see the bare soil, black rocks, the narrow fissures of the ravines. Madly the storm twisted this grey mane! Out of it came an immense rustling; the trunks of the trees, before hidden by the frothing leaves, were bared now by the wind's furious blasts; one could see their frail grey limbs as taut as a ship's rigging. And they yielded, they yielded—a dry crackling was the prelude to the fall, then suddenly a thousand cracklings could be heard, a cascade of resounding noises drowned by the howling of the storm, and the giants were engulfed. Now the shower let loose the icy chill of its deluge like the brutal volley of handfuls of pebbles, and the forest answered with the metallic reverberation of its myriad leaves. Bare rocks glinted like ominous cuirasses, the liquid yellowish splendour of the wet fog crowned for an instant the crest of each forest tree, for an instant a yellow and luminous and marvellously translucid band shone along the horizon against which every branch of every tree stood silhouetted, and made the drenched stones of the parapet, Albert's blond hair soaked by the rain, the cold wet fog rolling around the tops of the trees, shine with a golden gleam, icy and almost inhuman—then went out and night fell like the blow of an axe. The horrible violence of this savage nature, in an instant so different from what it had appeared at first, filled Albert's soul with sombre forebodings. Drenched with rain, he retraced his steps through the deserted rooms. The ruddy glow of a stained glass window, the far-off sound of a clock lost in some distant and lonely corridor made him shudder for a moment like a child. He shrugged his shoulders at these commonplace snares of terror but was, nonetheless, unable to shake off the weight of a persistent anxiety. Perhaps really *something had happened!* Turning the corner of a corridor his foot struck a sleeping form: it was the servant who had come to meet him, and who was now lying asleep, stretched out on the flagstones in the pose of an animal overwhelmed by a sickening fatigue—and involuntarily Albert shuddered. At last he reached the heart of that anxiety with which all afternoon he had been investing the landscape, and deservedly no doubt in many respects. In the middle of the great drawing-room a square of paper lay on a copper tray. He broke the seal of the message and read: "I shall arrive at Argol Friday. Heide will come with me."

II

THE GRAVEYARD

THE DAYS THAT FOLLOWED were for Albert, like
vacation days, capricious and profound. He was
as pleased as a child with his mysterious dwelling
and gave himself up to the charm of virgin nature.
Brittany was lavish with her meagre seductions, her
humble flowers: gorse, broom and heather covered
the moors over which Albert took interminable rides
on horseback every day.

Sometimes a heavy shower surprised him in the
midst of this countryside; he sought refuge in poor
granite huts, under *dolmens* thickly overgrown with
moss. Only into the forest of Storrvan he dared not
venture, and the terror that the storm on the evening
of his arrival had awakened in him still persisted in
his heart.

He nevertheless worked ardently deciphering the
difficult pages of that *Logic* from which the whole
Hegelian system seems to rise on august and angelic
wings. For the myths that have cradled humanity
throughout its long history, Albert had always evinced
abounding curiosity, searched passionately for their
secret significance; and one morning he was surprised to find that Hegel, in spite of his professed

aversion to examples, had seen fit to give an explanation of the myth of the Fall of man:

"Examining more closely the story of the Fall we find, as we have said, that it exemplifies the universal bearings of knowledge upon the spiritual life. In its instinctive and natural form, spiritual life wears the garb of innocence and trustful simplicity: but the very essence of spirit implies the absorption of this immediate condition into something higher. Spiritual life is distinguished from natural life, and more especially from animal life, in that it does not continue a blind fact, but rises to the consciousness of itself, and a being of its own. This division must in its turn vanish and be absorbed, and then the spirit can open up the victorious road to peace again. The concord then is spiritual; that is, the principle of restoration is found in thought, and thought alone. *The hand that inflicts the wound is also the hand that heals it.*"

From these pages seemed to wing a glorious certainty. Surely only knowledge and not a humiliating and human love, that Albert had always succeeded in killing through defiance, could reconcile him lastingly with himself; and if he were not deceiving himself, thus it must be: "You shall be as Gods, having knowledge of good and evil." That was the cause of the Fall, but also, it was the only possible redemption.

And he read again: "Spirit is not pure instinct; on the contrary, it implies essentially the tendency toward reasoning and meditation. Childish innocence has, no doubt, much charm and sweetness, but only because it reminds us of what the spirit must succeed in conquering for itself." This magnificent dialectic seemed like an answer from on high to Albert's disquietudes. Thus one could be freed only by knowledge, essential, living knowledge: Albert scanned with his mind's eye his studious and sequestered life, and now proudly felt himself completely vindicated. But could it be that these new and wild surroundings, to which his life had been transferred, had already so strongly worked on the *romantic* fibres of his heart that he now felt the necessity of justifying to himself his way of life? This rejoinder of his mind seemed to him presumptuous, and for a few moments, with rapid strides, he paced the terrace to and fro.

With Herminien's arrival, Albert would once more meet his most cherished friend. In him a never-failing ease of manner, a perfect aplomb, a genius for human intrigue captivated Albert, who was ever too inclined toward the heights, too given to flights into obscure and intoxicating regions that had won him the nickname—and he could still hear Herminien's deep and dubious voice pronouncing it—of "Doctor Faust." Especially surprising in Herminien was his singular aptitude for throwing light on the most obscure motives in human conduct. The recollection of long and subtle conversations, often continued until dawn in his high student's room where the light would hang like a belated star above the street, or in a country inn where, in the middle of a rambling cross-country walk, fatigue would stay them, conversations in which each with perfect good faith would try truthfully to get nearer to his own most hidden nature in a sort of dialogued confession, one mind, to take flight, continually seeking the support of the other mind, attentive and understanding, now brought back to Albert the imminent sensation of that faculty of double sight.

It had always seemed to him that Herminien made use of—and would always make use of—his unflagging power of analysis with perfect nonchalance and unconcern. Perhaps the bonds attaching him to life appeared to be lacking in strength, for his curiosity, manifold and always probing, was being forever dissipated. Sometimes it was the incomparable execution of certain rare paintings that took him through the museums of Europe, sometimes a woman was, for an instant, the pole of that avid human magnetism; Herminien would involve her in a whirlwind of intrigues in which insoluble complications seemed to spring up, as by enchantment, at every step. But these intrigues, at the very moment when they seemed to be assuming a fatal character, had invariably been brought to an abrupt halt, for Herminien, at the very moment his partner was to make her entrance upon the heroic stage where the whole setting complicitly encouraged drama and prompted the projection of her ardent passion, knew to perfection how to use the weapon of detached and sarcastic irony which he would skilfully handle, as an arm or as a charm, and which up until now, no tragic passion had been able to withstand. These extravagant games of mind and heart which he was constantly proposing and whose insignificance, at every instant, was emphasized by his marvellously natural attitude, left a lasting resentment in all the women invited to play a role, which he himself delineated at every moment in its slightest details.

Herminien possessed the gift of penetrating the secrets of literature and art with subtle and perfect taste, revealing, however, their mechanism rather than all the power of the grace they contained. And yet an enthusiasm, a cold susceptibility, a veritable exaltation was apparent in these perilous exercises: his calm expression would become animated, his eye luminous, physical fatigue would be without a hold on this body of steel, and discussion or analysis could be prolonged without effort on his part for whole days and nights at a time, until a logical conclusion had been reached. In the very core of his being, in his most febrile moments, an impenetrable reserve and a demoniac lucidity were ever present. Perhaps Albert was mistaken in gracing with the name of friendship a relationship which, everything considered, was extremely dubious, and which by the almost exact similarity of their tastes, by their way of broaching the ambiguities of language, and by a system of values, belonging to themselves alone, which ever present, but like an invisible thread, ran through every conversation they carried on in the presence of a third person, deserved rather the qualification, in every respect more disturbing, of complicity. So many curious tastes enjoyed in common, ritualistic perversions of a language of their own, mutually taught, ideas fashioned by the repeated shock of their rapier-like minds, signals given by an inflection of the voice too often exchanged, a reference to a book, a melody, a name bringing with it a whole throng of common recollections, had in the end created between them a dangerous, intoxicating, vibratile atmosphere, dissipated and reborn by their contact like the withdrawal and approach of the plates of an electric condenser.

Placed at this human focal point, every object appeared in a new and menacing light: the reverberation of words, the flashing of beauty engendered abnormal and prolonged vibrations, as though the proximity of this human charge in suspense, heavy and immobile, had brought all phenomena to their supreme degree of *explosion*, to their most immediate and frenzied consequences. And both of them for a long time now had been unconsciously feeding on this vitiated air, delicious and subtler than that of other men—the *human condenser* seemed to be born from the reunion of these two merging figures who with the darting rapidity of lightning seemed constantly pointing out to each other all the delirium of the fever and the danger.

The gifts of life, the gifts of beauty, the most enthralling experiences had no longer any value for either of them until brought into the full light of this double reflector which then penetrated them with its magic rays; they had even, perhaps, reached the point where they could *no longer* enjoy any prey until they had dragged it to their common lair, could not *see* with their individual eyes any human thing, which they could then penetrate like an empty crystal, until the other had lent the screen of his intimate and redoubtable hostility. For they were enemies too, but they dared not admit it. *They dared not admit it to each other*, nor tolerate the remotest suggestion that a relationship in any way strange could exist between them. Perhaps Hegel would have smiled to see, walking by the side of each, like a dark and glorious angel, the phantom both of his double and his contrary, and would then have ruminated on the form of this necessary *union* which this book must needs have as its goal—among others—finally to elucidate. Thus they walked, side by side and silent, mingling their exquisite taste for death whose near and enigmatic image each in turn reflected in the frenzies of a life that was *what they shared*.

Of the figure of Heide, Albert knew almost nothing. Spasmodic rumours, and until now unverifiable, pointed to the invariable coincidence of the arrival of Heide in any part of the globe with violent revolutionary outbreaks, abnormally numerous in these last few years, especially in the peninsulas of the Mediterranean and in America, and according to many it would seem that only in the atmosphere of such social upheavals, could this soul of ice and fire find its natural rhythm. Furthermore, during the last few weeks there had been an almost total silence on the subject of Heide, and now Albert realized with a strange feeling of uneasiness that in all these confused political rumours to which, as to all such preoccupations, he had lent an absent ear, he had never given a thought to the *sex* of his future guest, which the name Heide alone was not sufficient to elucidate, and that, up to the very moment of this enigmatic person's arrival, it would remain a mystery.

The day of this arrival, a pale sun shone over the

country of Argol, and Albert started out on horse-back for a long ride in the direction of the sea which from the castle towers he had seen shimmering in the distance. He took a path that ran along the edge of the valley between moss-covered cliffs on one side, and on the other a veritable wall of verdure whose long flexible green branches the indefatigable wind from the sea kept brushing against the rocks, as the neighbouring waves might have tossed pale forests of seaweed against the reefs, so that the path was entirely overhung by a dense bower of leaves through which the sun set a flickering maze of dazzling spots dancing along the ground. The path came out on to a desolate beach.

The last vestiges of life in this region seemed to be the long grey grasses whose thin whistling tufts clung untidily to the dunes and were matted together like long sea-drenched tresses by the gusts of wind. To the east, the view was arrested by a high black promontory. This sea, where neither bird nor sail met the eye which swept in an instant its vast expanse, seemed to him particularly unbearable in its mortal *vacuity*, for remaining a dull greyish white under a radiant sky, its surface perfectly rounded whose curve the glance involuntarily followed, irresistibly evoked the image of an eyeball whose pupil had rolled back into the socket leaving only the hideous dull white visible so that it was the entire surface which *looked*, and posed for the soul the most intolerable of questions. Not far out in the watery element, thin white lines, which seemed to duplicate the complicated festoons of the contours of the bay, advanced at intervals silently toward the shore: soon the ear was surprised by the noise as of a crashing wall of water, and then a wide wet tongue like the cool rough tongue of an ox, licked the sand with a rasping sound.

At the other end of the bay, where the wretched grasses gave place to naked beaches, Albert urged his horse toward a melancholy assemblage of worn grey stones fashioned by the hand of man and which, as he drew nearer, seemed to all appearances, to be a graveyard long since abandoned. The invading sands had already reached the level of the stone wall, and seemed to have completely filled the mortuary enclosure. Massive stone crosses with strangely short arms like those of Gaelic crosses emerged from the sand without any apparent order, and barely visible mounds still indicated the site of the graves. The wild desolation of this place, abandoned by man, inspired in Albert no more than a morbid curiosity, and tying his horse to the arm of one of the crosses, he walked rapidly along the paths smothered in sand. Not an inscription was any longer legible, and the agent of this pitiless and twofold sacrilegious destruction was revealed by the incessant whistling of grains of sand that the wind with horrible ferocity kept hurling in a fine dust against the granite. It seemed to flow from *His* inexhaustible palm, from the horrible palm of the sandman Time!

Albert's pale face now grew paler, and the wind madly tossed the locks of his blond and so strangely lustreless hair, which was the colour of ripe oats and of sand. His gaze was arrested by a stone cross planted a little apart from the others, and that seemed, as far as could be judged from the uneven inroads of the sand, quite notably higher than the others. But what struck Albert as peculiarly disquieting about the situation of this particular cross, was that no swelling of the ground, such as mournfully accounted for the presence of the other emblems of redemption in this deserted spot, was apparent in its vicinity where nothing could be seen but the uneven striations of the sand, so that the soul long hesitated to decide whether this cross, like the others, was the sign of Death, lying in the earth at its feet, or whether, on the contrary, it confronted this sleeping people of the graves with the proud image of eternal Life, present even in the midst of these funereal solitudes.

Little by little the enigma of this gibbet, equivocal and available, took possession of his mind, and with some force guiding his arm, while the almost insane smile, brought to his lips by some mysterious comparisons still lingered, he walked quickly toward the cross, and picking up a sharp piece of stone, roughly engraved on it the name of

HEIDE

A cloud at that moment hung heavily over the graveyard, and Albert threw back his head as much to enjoy a final look at the splendour of the bay as to discover the cause of this sudden eclipse. An enormous cloud was sailing slowly over the expanse of sea like a compassionate visitor to those watery plains unknown to any ship. Nothing can describe the slow and prodigal majesty with which this celestial navigation was accomplished. For a moment it seemed to proceed toward the farthest end of the bay, then, making a solemn turn, it veered toward the east, displaying like an aerial sailing vessel the contrast of the pure and dazzling whiteness of its swelling side with the deep gulfs of shadow that opened in its bosom. For an instant its huge bulk wavered over the graveyard illuminating with its stormy, pure and regal stateliness this landscape of death, then passed on, and an instant later the incessant whistling of the wind in the dry grasses, and the monotonous and muffled stamping of a horse's hoofs in the sand, were the only signs of life left on the deserted shore.

III

HEIDE

ALBERT SPENT the whole of the following day in the study he had arranged for himself in the highest tower of the castle from which his eyes could plunge into the forest. His mind was occupied with vague and indistinct reveries: more than ever, on the eve of this awaited visit, the forest seemed to him to be multiplying its retreats, to reveal flashes of mysterious comings and goings; an imminent presence pervaded it like an airy living thing, of which the glitter of the leaves seemed to Albert the symbolic evidence. The empty rooms of the castle in their drowsy torpor waited for this presence to people them, and the sound of footsteps on the flags, a creaking of the oaken wainscot, the thud of a bee against a windowpane echoed in the recesses of the brain like a signal, long and eagerly awaited. And Albert had the curious feeling that this somnolent castle *must* be *visited* or perish, like a castle of legend, burying the enigmatic sleeping servants under its ruins. During the hot hours of the afternoon the waiting became more intolerable with every second, in the midst of an idleness that delivered up the defenceless soul to all the terrors of midday. Toward evening two tall figures appeared

41

on the path leading to the castle, and Albert, whose heart seemed to stop beating with excitement and apprehension, hastened down to meet his guests.

He and Herminien greeted each other in the most formal manner. Those broad shoulders, every feature of that sun-tanned face, the vigorously planted hair, the deep tones of voice so resonant in the lofty stone hall, all proclaimed contentment and a visible plenitude. While they exchanged commonplace phrases singularly devoid of expression, a third person, without effort, appropriated all the interest of the scene from which banality was instantly and effectively banished. In a flash, Heide filled the room, the castle and the whole region of Argol with her radiant and absorbing beauty.

She appeared to be entirely dressed in white fabrics of a remarkably delicate workmanship—with ample folds, among which her pink hands fluttered. Her face was as various as the hours of the day and the different planes were so composed as to seem like a prism in which each ray of light that touched it remained imprisoned and radiated a soft lustre through the skin, a living crystallization of light. Even the eyes, in which poets have been wont to see the only human reflection of the heavens, shone with scarcely a brighter glow in that face behind which light seemed to flow through invisible and translucent vessels.

All ordinary notions of beauty commonly associated with proportion and line had to be abandoned the minute one sought to appreciate the inimitable radiance of this countenance which seemed destined to render strikingly apparent, even to the most untutored eyes, the distinction of *quality* and of *degree*. And because pure quality reigned mistress there, independent of all questions of proportion, and consequently of appraisement, one instinctively sought in music the elements of comparison for this scarcely terrestrial face: no painter, no poet, without a secret sense of *ridicule*, would have attempted to render its supernatural radiance—but, on the contrary, it was to certain rare and profoundly ambiguous melodic contours, particularly to certain almost incantatory phrases of *Lohengrin*—where the intolerable glare of a sword seems by its glitter to thwart the warmest and most nostalgic sonorities—that the mind turned, as a last resort, in its attempt to assimilate a beauty before which the judgment had from the first capitulated—and which must forever leave one helpless and without appeal, in that, even before it had been perceived, it was felt to be *unique*.

Try as he might to elucidate the ties—totally unsuspected by him until today—that might exist between Herminien and Heide, or to explain the reasons for this double visit, they remained inscrutable. Slowly he and his guests strolled through the rooms of the castle which now, for the first time, revealed to Albert a remarkable property, for their unprecedented and always varied dimensions through a baffling acoustics, regulated the tones of the speakers' voices, and the conversation, bright and gay in the apartments filled with sunlight, lent to the metallic resonance of the copper plaques in the dining-room a sharp and sparkling sonority like the clash of arms, while in the drawing-room, muffled by the half-light and the height of the vaulted ceiling, it fell to a murmur, faint and intensely musical.

Having seated themselves around the massive copper table, their conversation gradually took on a profounder tone and an accelerated tempo. Heide now gave proof, not only of a very surprising culture, but even of an extensive *learning*, which astonished Albert. The most discerning and original views were combined in her with an absence—apparent but, for all that, difficult to fathom—of all the most universally accepted moral and social prejudices. And yet an evident modesty was continually being restored to her by her fantastic beauty: and it seemed that these social laws which she thus ignored were easy enough for her to abolish in a world over which she was willingly accorded omnipotent power, but which must, nevertheless, be resuscitated, and were all the more fatal for a being whose *privileged* state seemed, in spite of herself, to give rise to a thousand unknown and menacing interdictions. Thus she remained, in the midst of the most daring and dangerous utterances, lofty, inaccessible, and redoubtable—and no matter how passionately she sought to *explain* and, without the least embarrassment to reveal herself to her inter-locutors, her character seemed every moment to become only more completely unknowable. In the mysteries of her beauty, seemingly projected outside herself and surrounding her like impalpable veils, she was ceaselessly buried and reborn with the lustre of total newness, crossing and recrossing a magic threshold forbidden to men, like the forever inviolable curtain of a theatre, and behind which she provided herself with new arms, daggers, philters and impene-trable cuirasses.

For Albert and Herminien the bonds, *indefinable* in spite of everything, and of which the reader has been sufficiently apprised, were renewed by this fresh meet-ing with a swiftness and a violence all the greater now that a setting perfectly designed to arouse all sorts of disquieting sensations lent its dangerous com-plicity. Through all the detours of a sprightly con-versation—to which the presence of Heide added a perilous attraction—their only object, in spite of all appearances, was to effect a mutual *reconnaissance*, to reconstruct and, with acute delight, to make each other touch the infinitely sinuous line of demarcation which the shock, so often repeated, of these two natures had long ago fixed in ideal space where they took refuge. They looked for and found each other! Finally, with a rapture they hardly dared admit, they recognized certain ambiguous glances, certain perfidious insinuations—the intention hidden in a certain over-emphasis studiously humorous, even the drawling pronunciation of a certain vowel became for them significant: all the most complex subtleties of the game were tried with a supreme nonchalance and, at the first signal, easily understood—the dubious alliance was again perfect, and this league, stronger than any vows, presented an unbroken front to the world whose attacks it scorned—diabolic and indissoluble to such a degree that each one's most spontaneous thoughts being instantaneously caught by the other in their total *interiority* seemed, even to the most innocent eyes, to bear the indubitable mark of conspiracy.

Meanwhile, little by little, the sun in its decline flooded the room with its almost horizontal rays, crowned Heide's blond hair with a golden aureole and for the space of a second lent her the overwhelming importance that the *contre-jour* gives to figures in a living scene no less than to those in Rembrandt's works—the eyes of Albert and Herminien, drawn in spite of themselves to the centre of this luminous phantasmagoria, met for the space of a lightning flash—and understood. *Something had changed.*

The strangeness of their dialogue which had in the last few minutes taken on an accelerated, an almost fantastic pace, the limpidity of the mechanism of their minds which seemed to function without the least effort at a quadruple speed, the sparkling quality of the words exchanged without respite which had seemed to devour the hours of the evening like a flame revived by an incessant flow of oxygen—of all this, with anguished stupefaction, they took cognizance, attributing it to its veritable cause. The setting sun now forced their attention on this effect of light: it suddenly acquired complete ascendancy over their taut nerves—as over the pilgrims the ray of light with which Rembrandt envelops his Christ—and Heide now seemed indicated, more surely than by the pointing finger of destiny, as the origin of this singular alteration in their relations which can only be understood by analogy with the phenomenon which physicists call catalysis.

A perceptible break now occurred in the conversation, followed by painful and desultory talk, scarcely heeded by either of them, each being preoccupied in trying to fathom the possible consequences of an event hardly less extraordinary than would have seemed the sudden crumbling of the castle about their heads. An embarrassment, growing every second more intolerable and which seemed to hover over the table like a thunder cloud, followed their discovery—buried by each on the instant in the depths of his heart—and Albert, to mitigate by any sort of interruption the throbbings of that heart which from now on it would be impossible to quiet altogether, led Heide to the upper terraces.

The moon flooded the whole landscape with a heady loveliness. Night lavished her treasures. In the sky each star took its place with the same exactitude as on a sidereal chart, and presented such an authentic image of *night*, as one had always known and had a right always to expect, that the heart was touched by this scrupulous, naïve, and almost childish reconstruction, as by an act of unfathomable beneficence. Night lavished her treasures. The air was deliciously cool. And as Heide and Albert reached the edge of the stone parapet suddenly they were both at the same moment seized by a strange emotion. As though bathed by the glow of footlights, the round heads of the trees everywhere loomed out of the abyss, huddled together in silence, risen out of the abyss of silence surrounding the manor like a people conjured up by darkness, who had assembled and were waiting for the *three strokes* to resound from the castle towers. This mute, motionless, obstinate waiting overwhelmed the heart which could *not possibly* fail to respond to this mad, this marvellous hope.

Pale, both of them, they stood there on the high terrace, and caught thus in the ray of the moon's gaze and of the forest's, they dared not withdraw. Nor dared they look at each other, for suddenly everything took on an aspect of unaccountable gravity. They knew not what was to become of them, nor anything of what would be decided for them. And the night resembled them! Then Heide with a shudder of her whole being (no doubt, as a woman, she was less invincibly timid, and no doubt Albert was not in love with her) laid on Albert's hand her hand, as cold as marble and as hot as fire; with the slowness of torture, with force and frenzy, she twined each one of her fingers in his, and drawing his face to hers, she forced him to take her lips in a prolonged kiss that shook her entire body as though lightning had passed through it. And now, as they went down the stairs, along the corridors, through all the lugubrious darkness of the empty castle—they could not free their hearts of the appalling weight of the *event*.

Left alone, Herminien sat lost in gloomy and absorbing thought, to which, little by little, the monotonous ticking of a massive copper clock ornamenting one corner of the room—and that had grown suddenly loud and strangely noticeable since the departure of the other two—lent a character of inexorable fatality. His nerves quivered as the pendulum with each succeeding second aggravated to a horrifying extent the duration of this inexplicable disappearance. With melancholy insistence Herminien's mind followed Albert and Heide through all the devious windings of the castle. Certainly this dinner, apparently so commonplace, could not have failed to provide him with a quantity of passionate and, no doubt, torturing observations—which he now recapitulated in detail with hallucinating precision—which his devastatingly lucid mind unrolled before him through all their infinitely changing and yet wholly significant mazes. How could the too visible signs of interest, which Heide had never for an instant ceased to show for Albert, have escaped him!—but now he discerned their fatal character as well.

The fabulous atmosphere in which this lonely countryside, this sequestered domain, enveloped such a manifestly romantic figure, the curious detachment Albert had shown toward Heide throughout the dinner while he engaged Herminien in a dialogue whose *inner* character must have intrigued to the highest degree a naturally dominating mind—all this might have, must have, awakened in Heide a passionate interest, growing stronger with each passing second, for Herminien's friend. She had hitherto only known Herminien in his isolation, in his relative *poverty*, and she must have attributed the cause of this sudden fulguration, this feverish, electric atmosphere, invariably recreated at each conjunction of these two polarizing figures, and in whose effluvium she had felt herself bathed all evening, to Albert alone—and for a being whose native freedom and abrupt impulses, which he well knew, this could not have have failed to mark the beginning of a fanatical passion. And while the clock, second by second, ticked away the fragments of an hour that seemed suddenly charged for Herminien with a richer substance and stamped with a character, above all else, *irremediable*, a bitter, unfinished smile— at the same time contradicted by an expression of intense reflection—played over his lips.

This double absence at last afforded him an opportunity to turn his attention—until now violently taken up by the other actors on the stage—to himself, and the singularly unjustifiable character of this journey to Argol which he had undertaken with Heide, now became apparent, together with its true, its overwhelming significance. He had to admit that an instinct, certainly very different from that of self-preservation, had governed his conduct ever since he had known Heide, believing from the first that he felt for this, in every respect, most singular being a complete personal detachment. And it was perhaps at this instant that he realized for the first time that in every human being the instinct for self-destruction, for devastating self-immolation, constantly wars, and no doubt with unequal arms, with his concern for his own safety. Certainly he might well have imagined in advance what would be—what could not fail to be—Heide's feeling for Albert, but apart from a perhaps morbid curiosity, he thought he could now detect in his conduct a much more disconcerting motive, and this sudden realization burst like an access of fever in his brain.

What *he could not have known in advance* was what Heide would become for him at Argol, and yet he did not hesitate to raise a question that involved nothing less than his whole peace of mind. And he now felt—and the full consciousness of it beat against his brain like the wings of madness itself—that he had brought her to Albert in order to plunge her into the heart of their double life, to kindle her with the blaze of a light unknown to men, which had constituted his whole life until now—in order that, marked with the sign of this indelible sacrament, she should henceforth become for him more completely close, more inseparable than his own pulse-beat. Thus, with startling rapidity, his mind in its eagle flight effected this decisive *circuit of the horizon* that finally closed on itself with the conclusive click of a sprung trap, and the night, which had now established her empire around the living heart of the castle, seemed to him to close the last exits, one by one.

IV

HERMINIEN

VIGILANT, THE SOLITUDES encompassing the castle closed around the visitors, whose sojourn soon seemed destined to take on the aspect of indefinite duration.

As for Heide, she felt herself to be at one of those *nodes* of the planet's human vibrations where absolute calm, albeit engendered by the juggling interference of contrary motions, is all the more soothing in its perilous instability—and nature now appeared to her in the light of a seductive and inexhaustible freshness—with animal unconsciousness she feasted on the sharp and stimulating air, the sparkle of grass and trees, the purity of living waters. She seemed clothed in freshness and in innocence. A spring, a grove of oaks, a sunlit clearing were the goals of her unpremeditated excursions, from which all strictly human incentive seemed momentarily excluded. She haunted the woods of Storrvan, the ocean's shores where her dramatic appearances rivalled the rarest spectacles of this world of virgin nature filled with the play of living water and of the wind, on whose wings with marvellous majesty she abandoned the folds of her long white cape.

Life flowed ardently through her limbs, beloved of the light, which ceaselessly bathed them in a delicate vapour. The presence of Albert seemed to her to extend to the extreme limits of his enchanted domain, to such a point that more than once the invigorating virtue of his adored body seemed even nearer to her and more real beside some cool spring, in some un-explored forest retreat, than on the terrace the first evening when she had offered him that kiss whose temerity filled her with an enduring stupefaction.

Their life together fell naturally into a succession of distinct and barely real scenes like those of a play in which the purely interior character of the drama is emphasized by the extremely restricted number of the cast. It generally happened that during the first half of the day each actor was left to his own devices in com-plete independence, as in the *exposition* of a play each character is first presented to the audience in all his freshness, still untrammelled by the plot which grows ever more fatal and gradually sets a sinister restriction on each of his slightest gestures up to the final cata-strophe of the play.

Thus, the mornings were often consecrated to soli-tary walks to the sea or in the forest, and the spell of the sunlight, all the blooming freshness that seemed to be presiding over a new creation of the earth rising out of chaos, with insidious malignity made each of them believe that life was once more open before them, free of all hindrance; they breathed in deep draughts of this recreated air of the childhood of the earth, their minds seemed to grow virginal, seemed, in their exciting liberty, to have escaped without difficulty from the influence of the subtle atmosphere which the storm of the first evening had left stagnating around the castle like the nitrous odour that lingers after an electric discharge. But in all this an initiated mind would see only a refinement of fate which lavished these treacherous consolations upon them just as wine is mixed with aromatic spices to fortify bodies under torture, in order to intensify the sharpness of fresh torments and make the victim feel to the full the excruciating bliss. In the afternoon, a torpor that the sun let fall heavily over the courts and apartments of the castle, warned their nerves, on edge with waiting, of the prelude to a deadly game. Some force drew Heide and Albert together, and for endless hours they would disappear, would lose themselves in the nearby forest in a perilous tête-à-tête. These aimless excursions through the forest soon acquired for them both an irremediable charm. It now seemed to Heide that, at every instant, the world died and was reborn to the joint reverberation of their footsteps, and that, light and vacillating, her whole life hung on Albert's arm.

But an uneasiness soon followed these moments of abandon. All her blood would stir, awaken in her, filling her arteries with an overwhelming ardour, like a purple tree sending out its shoots in the heavenly shade of the forest. She became a motionless column of blood, and a monstrous anguish awoke in her; it seemed to her that her veins could not contain another instant the appalling flow of this blood which leapt in her furiously at the mere touch of Albert's arm, and that it was about to gush forth and spatter the trees with its hot jet, while she would be seized by the chill of death whose dagger point she seemed already to feel plunged between her shoulder blades. Then, trembling, she would drop Albert's arm, would lie down on the moss at his feet and hide her head in her arms, not yet willing to let him read in the depths of her eyes her crushing defeat. And while he stood leaning against the low branch of a tree, turning toward her the brightness of his lucid and cruel eyes, she, in surrender and angelic trust—like a wholly submissive slave—offered him like a prayer the treasures of her body utterly dedicated to him.

She untied her sandals and her bare feet glistened on the cool carpet of moss. Under the light silk of her dress the palpitation of her breasts was barely perceptible. She loosened her hair and let it spread like a pool around her on the grass. She stretched

out her arms and the warm muscles trembled with
the ardour of an enchanted life. At last she turned her
eyes toward him and let a viscid glow filter through
them even like the veil of blood it traversed. She lay
there before him wholly offered up to the one from
whom, with every instant, she drew the miracle of
the prolongation of her life, and it seemed to her at
times that a mass of molten metal of a consuming
heat was born from her swelling tortured breasts,
and filled the caverns of her flesh with floods of liquid fire; at others, deliriously light she felt herself
lifted and inhaled by the blue and distant sky which
was like a well of cool light through the tops of the
trees above her. And such was the explosion of life
within her that it seemed to her that her body in the
consuming heat was about to open like a ripe peach,
and her skin in all its massive thickness to be torn
from her, turned inside out toward the sun to exhaust
the fires of love in all her red arteries, and that her
most secret flesh as well would be torn out of her
very depths in quivering shreds, and burst through
all her thousand recesses like a banner of blood and
flame flashing in the face of the sun in a final inex-
pressible and appalling nudity.

But although his heart weighed all the compassion
of such a surrender, Albert remained insensible. Did
he, perhaps, despise a triumph for which he had not

contended, feel chagrined that his will was held at
nought by capricious fortune who surrendered into
his hands with the irony of total *gratuitousness*, the
most ravishing of creatures? But above all it seemed
to him impossible that Heide, of all people, could
admit a solution of such equivocal facility—that the
possession of this splendid and surrendered body
might be—from any point of view whatsoever—the
solution. He looked at Heide lying at his feet—and
straightway another image rose before him with
haunting persistence: he saw once more the castle
towers around which dusk's melancholy shadows were
falling just as, at the turn of the path, the two white
figures of Heide and Herminien, heads bowed, lips
tightly closed over an indecipherable message, appeared in the hermetic silence of their fabulous
arrival—and the absurdity, the impossibility of re-
conciling these two images grew ever more irresistible.
And he saw Heide again as she was to appear at the
table later that evening, dramatic and unreal like a
princess in a play—behind the ramparts of her invi-
olate beauty—he heard again the subtle words he
had exchanged with Herminien whose stimulating
presence *permitted him to see her* for the first time—and
the idea that she should, that she could, make him
the gift of herself seemed to him a particularly gross
and reprehensible subterfuge, although its exact nature

still escaped him. Then addressing Heide in terms of a tender and henceforth inseparable friendship, he led her back to the castle where Herminien was waiting for them.

Those long evenings which they spent together in closest intimacy, little by little, came to be for Albert the only moment of the day when he felt he could relish his life in all its *plenitude*. As soon as Heide and Herminien were together, Albert became palpably aware of that agonizing secret something that he seemed to divine between them and that had given such a startling radiance to their presence that first evening as they stood at the castle door. And so now, to every word, to every glance that was exchanged between them, his ears and his eyes attributed some magnetic virtue; and he sought to surprise the inviolable *secret* they seemed, at the moment, to be communicating to each other. It seemed to him that Heide, so close to him, and so utterly abandoned to his mercy during the afternoon, now escaped him as though responding to a magnetic call, as though under some urgent, superior, and secret obligation. Toward her Herminien affected an invariably courteous and reserved manner, from which even a certain coldness was not absent, but at the same time Albert was aware of a ferocious *irony* shining in his eyes as they lazily turned from Heide to him, from him to Heide, and the mere suspicion of such an irony made him erect between himself and Herminien a solid wall of hostility. Heide, stimulated perhaps by a sort of regal state that her sex conferred upon her in the presence of these two men, shone brilliantly in the conversation, and a sort of superior *coquetry* that appeared in her seemed the complaisant result of a situation in which every advantage was hers, rather than that of any personal contribution on her part. Every gesture and the bright music of her words bore the accent of triumph, and at moments the eyes of her two interlocutors would turn toward her with an identical movement, as though to pay her an involuntary homage. Then their eyes would meet, and a hostility, very different from the uneasiness of the glance exchanged on that first evening, might be read in them.

And sometimes it happened in the conduct of these evenings that it was Herminien in his turn who assumed the directing role, the character of which was particularly intolerable to Albert. It consisted in implying by his words—and more especially by his delicate *reticences* and an affected care not to *embarrass* them by too direct allusions—that there existed between Heide and Albert a subtle and unusual relationship. And then his courteous, smiling glance, as it turned from one to the other, seemed to be mocking them, and in the most offensive way to be excusing them as though to place himself on a superior plane of intelligence. And to Albert it seemed then that Herminien really held them in his hands, that he recreated them, manipulated them, twisted them together according to his fancy—tangled them and untangled them at his leisure—so perfect was the subtle play of his allusions and of his infinitely shaded reservations. He seemed to invest them with a guilty poetry, to attribute to them a thousand illicit entanglements, enveloping them with a palpable air of conspiracy, and in Albert, who well knew the excessive and, for him, insipid simplicity of the passion that had been awakened in Heide for him, a deep anger arose before this veritable creation that Herminien presented each evening, before what must appear to him a despicable expropriation. With an insufferable ease and detachment it seemed to him that Herminien —whom fate was apparently keeping so completely out of the game—brought together these ties—so easily explicable in themselves when unrelated to him—simply by his gift of comprehension, invention, and intrigue.

And the extreme *poverty* of Albert's sentiments for Heide, made him each night the helpless victim of Herminien's imagination—for he perceived that he could now *no longer* get along without seeing *represented* every evening for him and to his furious stupefaction, the masterpiece that Herminien like a magician stage director, in the course of the conversation and with the assistance of infinite art, would create out of the crude material that Heide and Albert in the afternoon seemed to have accumulated only for him. He could not now reject this iridescent, malignant, peerless translation that Herminien with nonchalant virtuosity, a tender and terrible connivance that silently referred to the years of blind complicity, offered him every evening when the reunion of these three strange actors gave the signal for the play to begin. He could not resist the reminder of such a long-tested alliance, and the delicate machinery as though polished by long use, a winged machine, seemed to be set in motion with fatal slowness and to drag him along after Herminien, with the insistence of a spell, toward an end for him, in every respect, unpredictable. Thus day by day proceeded this annexation, ceaselessly watched over by Herminien with the cold and cruelly fascinating eye of a dazzling reptile.

Herminien kept thinking of Heide. His days, which Albert supposed filled with the substance of rewarding work, with arduous meditations, were almost wholly spent lying on his bed, from which he could plunge his eyes into the melancholy woods of Storrvan. Hardly had he seen Heide's white skirt disappear through the nearest trees, than it seemed to him that life had gone from him and that the sun now shone over utterly arid horizons. Then, as a last resort, he would plunge his face into the cool darkness of his pillows, savagely biting the delicate white linen, and his pitilessly lucid mind would call up before him the image of Heide and Albert wandering together through the heart of the fragrant forest, for him rendered impenetrable by the most barbarous of enchantments; with his mind's eye he would follow the footsteps of the one whom he had brought here that he might realize her great price when she had been taken from him.

Then the swinging pendulum of the clock, with a poignant familiarity of the first evening, would remind him of the torture that each second until the hour of dinner held for him, an empty and altogether fantastic Time, whose horror consisted entirely in the differentiation, for the first time, of the course of its duration, a Time from which the passage of all really vital phenomena had completely vanished since Heide was now beyond his reach. But when in the great drawing-room of the castle, evening had restored for him the unity of a world that seemed to be completely contained within those walls, his mind was seized with a tremulous exaltation. With the fervour of semi-delirium, with a sort of vertiginous volubility, he now threw out his words like the meshes of a net in which he sought to envelop in a despairing embrace the woman who seemed henceforth separated from him by an atrocious malediction. To stay her, to hold her, to charm her he would have liked to fill the drawing-room and the entire manor with his dangerous arabesques, with his overpowering incantations, and with marvellously active vigilance, to stake out with his thoughts all the avenues that might be open to Heide's soul—to spread out his mind to the extreme limits of the world like a magic and living carpet covered with giant flowers, beyond which her foot would have no chance to stray. And with a sublime desperation, in the mad defiance of his heart, each evening was woven anew this Penelope's web, this spidery tissue that Heide, all unconscious, would instantly and easily rend, but whose thousand meshes Albert felt descending over him like a shadow over his brain.

V

THE SWIM

ONE MORNING when the light mist that lingered among the trees presaged the advent of a torrid day, they started out for a swim in the gulf, whose watery and eternally deserted wastes could be seen sparkling from the castle. A powerful car took them jolting over stony roads. The landscape, which had first appeared to Albert as so intensely dramatic, was now covered with a soft translucent mist. The air was full of a salty tingling freshness that came to them from the chasms of the sea, redolent of an odour headier than the smell of earth after rain: it seemed that each particle of skin simultaneously consumed all these profound delights, and if one closed one's eyes, the body suddenly to the senses had the form of a wine skin wholly closed around with warm darkness, whose marvellous living wall could be felt everywhere and at the same time by its contact with a coolness, no longer accidental but telluric, seeming to be radiated by all the pores of the planet, as its intolerable heat is radiated by the sun.

The driving wind from the sea in long smooth waves whipped their faces and tore from the damp sand a sparkling dust—and great sea birds with long wings seemed, by their jerky flights and sudden stops, to mark, like the sea, their ebb and flow on invisible beaches of the sky where, with outspread, motionless wings, they appeared to be stranded at times like white medusae. The wet shores were hidden by endless banks of fog which the unruffled sea, reflecting the almost horizontal rays of the sun, lighted from below with a powdery radiance, and the smooth streamers of mist could hardly be distinguished by the marvelling eye from the pools of water and the uniform expanses of wet sand—so in the morning of creation the charmed eye might have watched the unfolding of the naïve mystery of the *separation of the elements*.

They undressed among the graves. The sun burst through the mist, lighting the scene with its rays just as Heide in her dazzling nudity walked toward the sea with a step more mettlesome and light than that of a mare of the desert sands. In that shimmering landscape formed by those long watery reflections, in the omnipotent *horizontality* of those banks of mist, of those smooth flat waves, of those gliding rays of the sun, she suddenly startled the eye by the miracle of her *verticality*. All along the sun-devoured shore from which all shadows had fled, she set sublime reflections flowing. It seemed as though she were *walking on the waters*. In front of Herminien and Albert, whose eyes ran lingeringly over her strong, shadowy smooth back, over the heavy masses of her hair, and whose chests rose and fell to the marvellous slow rhythm of her legs, she stood out against the disc of the rising sun which sent streaming to her feet a carpet of liquid fire.

She raised her arms and without an effort, like a living caryatid, supported the sky on her hands. It seemed that the flow of that captivating and mysterious grace could not continue another instant without the vessels bursting in their perilously pounding hearts. Then she threw back her head, and in a frail sweet gesture raised her shoulders, and the foam that blew against her breasts and against her belly sent such an intolerably voluptuous sensation coursing through her that her lips drew back over her teeth in a passionate grimace—and to the surprise of the two spectators, at that instant there burst from this exultant figure the disordered and fragile movements of a woman.

Herminien, lingering on the shore, was transfixed by a tumultuous image. He was living over again that moment when the sun, breaking through the mists suddenly with its fiery darts, imprinted Heide in the depth of his heart—and those tragic moments when, with head thrown back between her shoulders as from too violent a shock, there escaped from her like an involuntary admission, the gestures of possession. Then her long and liquid eyes rolled back, her hands opened, each finger slowly unfolding as in the free surrender of a last resistance, her teeth glittered in the sunlight one by one in all their insolence, her lips parted like a wound henceforth impossible to conceal, her whole body trembled all through its solid thickness, and the toes rose as though all the nerves of the body were stretched to breaking point, like the rigging of a ship ravaged by an unknown wind.

They swam, the three of them, toward the high sea. Lying almost on the surface of the water, they watched the heavy waves come rolling toward them from the horizon in regular succession, and in the vertiginous tumult of their senses it seemed to them that the entire weight of the waters fell on their shoulders and must surely crush them—before forming beneath them a swell of softness and of silence which would lift them lazily on its weary back with a sensation of exquisite lightness. Sometimes the crest of a wave would brusquely throw its shadow over Heide's face, sometimes the salty gleam of her wet cheek would reappear. It seemed to them that, little by little, their muscles began to partake of the dissolving power of the element that bore them along: their flesh seemed to lose some of its density and to become identified, by an obscure osmosis, with the liquid meshes that entangled them. They felt a matchless purity, an incomparable freedom being born in them—they smiled, all three of them, a smile unknown to men, as they braved the incalculable horizon.

They were headed *out to sea*, and so many were the waves that had already rolled under them, so many the sudden and threatening crests they had breasted, and behind which appeared once more all the aridity of those plains, consecrated to the sun alone, that it seemed to them that the earth behind them must already have disappeared from sight, abandoning them to their enchanted migration in the midst of the waves. And with exultant cries, they encouraged each other in their flight. And it seemed to Albert that the water was actually *flowing* under them rushing at an unimaginable speed, and would overflow the melancholy shore, while he with his travelling companions pursued a voyage that, in his mind, increasingly took on the character of enchantment. They swam on and on at what seemed to them a constantly accelerated speed. A sharp challenge appeared in their eyes, gaining strength as they pursued this race without a goal. A few minutes more and, with the consciousness of the great distance already covered, an icy conviction became fixed in their minds. It seemed to them, to the three of them

71

at the same moment, that now they would *no longer* dare to turn back, would not dare to look toward the shore, and with a glance they exchanged a pledge that bound them body and soul.

Each of them seemed to see this mortal challenge in the others' eyes—to feel that the other two were sweeping him along by the whole force of their bodies and their wills—out to sea—further—toward unknown spaces—toward a gulf from which return would be impossible—and neither of them had any doubt as to the insidious character of this abrupt accord of their wills and of their destinies. *It was no longer possible to retreat.* They swam to rhythmic gasps escaping from their three chests, and with the thrilling chill of death the keen air penetrated their tired lungs. They looked lingeringly at one another. They could not detach their eyes one from the other, while lucidly their minds calculated the unretraceable distance already covered. And in a voluptuous transport, each recognized on the other faces the indubitable signs, the reflection of his own conviction, stronger with every second—now it was certain, they *would no longer have strength enough to return.*

And with a holy ardour they plunged forward through the waves, and in the joy of their peremptory discovery, at the price of their common death, every instant more inevitable, each yard gained redoubled their inconceivable felicity. And, beyond hate and beyond love, they felt themselves melting, all three of them, while they glided now with furious energy into the abyss—in one single vaster body, in the light of a superhuman hope that filled their eyes, drowned in blood and brine, with the reassuring peace of tears. Their hearts leaped in their breasts, and the very limit of their strength seemed now at hand—they knew that not one of them would break the silence, would ask to turn back—their eyes shone with savage joy. Beyond life and beyond death they now looked at one another for the first time with sealed lips, and through transparent eyes plumbed the darkness of their hearts with devastating bliss— and their souls touched in an electric caress. And it seemed to them that death would reach them, not when the swelling chasms beneath them should claim their prey, but when the lenses of their staring eyes— fiercer than the mirrors of Archimedes—should consume them in the convergence of an all-devouring communion.

Suddenly Heide's head disappeared under the water and all movement in her seemed to cease. Then Herminien, with a sudden shudder, *awoke* and out of his breast rose an astonishing cry. They plunged into the watery half-light. White shapes floated before their eyes as one or another of their limbs appeared,

73

slowly moving through the opaque greenness in which they seemed profoundly ensnared. Suddenly, in this submarine quest their eyes met, and seemed to touch, and they closed them with the sensation of an intolerable danger, as though confronted by the eye of the abyss itself, magnetic and hideous, engendering an icy dizziness.

In this frenzied search, during which it seemed to them that their hands brandished invisible knives, the form of a breast, as hard as stone, suddenly floated into Herminien's palm, then an arm which he seized with desperate violence, and when he opened his eyes above the surface of the water out of the choking terror that had surrounded him, he found the three of them reunited.

The sun blinded them like a flow of molten metal. Far away a yellowish line, thin and almost unreal, marked the beginning of that element which they had thought to have renounced forever. A spell was broken. They felt the earth's call, it echoed like an alarm bell, sounded deep in their muscles and in their brains. Anguish tightened around their temples, unnerved their hands; straining their wills to the uttermost, they swam towards land, and it seemed to them that they would never reach it now—the effort of their hands in the water seemed to be detached from them and like the dip of a useless oar. There was a burst of sunlight, and the whole bay was resplendent as for a melancholy celebration, a last irony of nature before their now inevitable end. Unendurably the blood tore like searing lightning through their brains.

But at last sand slipped under their feet; and with arms outflung they lay with all their weight, in mortal fatigue, on the wet beach, their eyes following the soothing movement of the clouds in the sky, and feeling all along their now supported limbs, the calm gladness of the earth. The wind caressed their faces and flew away like an insect from a flower, and they were astonished by the regular movement of the clouds, the agility of the grass, the noisy enthusiasm of the waves, and the mystery of their respiration that seemed to come to them like an unknown and charitable guest.

The hesitating spark of life wakened deeper and deeper zones of their flesh and, little by little, out of the mass of dense cold air, the clouds, and the penetrating humidity of the sand, like a statue out of its block of marble, they were born, they were detached. As in the morning of the world they expanded in the torrid heat of the sun, they began to stir on the sand and at last rising, they stood there erect on the shore, each surprised to assume again his own particular stature, surprised that life as it returned in its individual poverty, should hold out to them so quickly the decorous garments and the matrix of an ineluctable *personality*. But even now, still they *did not dare to speak*: had it been lost, drowned in the midst of the insatiable waves, the perverse secret of their hearts?

VI

THE CHAPEL OF
THE ABYSS

A FEW DAYS AFTER these signal events, Albert
strolled idly along the banks of the river of Argol.
These perilous gorges, these precipitous crags, veiled
in the thick curtain of the woods, attracted his tor-
mented soul. Here the river rolled its waters along
the bottom of a natural chasm with towering sides,
to which clung all the rich verdure of a glorious
forest. The continual windings of the river's course
gave an aspect of singular isolation to these retreats.
Around Albert the high walls of frowning forest
seemed to consume a considerable portion of the sky,
and even to touch the edge of the sun's ardent disc
although it had already risen high over the horizon.
These branches, majestically and rhythmically swaying, were stirred by the wind from the nearby sea
which brought with it the roar of the waves and the
aerial tumult of boundless space. But below this grandiose symphony, on a level with the stream, all was
stillness and untroubled calm in the shelter of the
impenetrable rampart of trees through which transparent and motionless columns of coolness rose from
the water.

Sometimes, struck by the slanting rays of the sun, the river in one of its broad sweeps burst on the eye with its wide beaches sparkling in the dazzling light, sometimes it contracted into a deep and narrow channel between high verdant walls, where it seemed to be escaping with the thick fluidity of oil, green and black, seemed to be *adapting itself* to the darkling hue of the high walls, with the guile of a natural snare that struck the senses with a silent horror, like a serpent gliding through the grass.

This natural ambush—with no possible escape for the soul goaded by mystery and curiosity and by the encompassing silence where no bird sang, and where the too apparent symptoms of the habitual lethargy of *night* were contradicted only by the altogether singular gaze of the white, vacant and blinding disc of the sun darting Albert's eye into the cool entrails of the earth—seemed the scene of an unfathomable crime where the utterly indisputable absence of any *piece of evidence* must finally attract the eye to the now altogether significant depths of those dark, transparent waters where, haunted by a sinister foreboding, his eye now sought a golden ring set with fabulous gems, or a dagger still smeared with a network of those red and indelible filaments that make the complete dilution of human blood in water forever so improbable.

The curious presence of the sun over that lofty horizon at a late hour of the afternoon (looking more like the moon in the middle of the night brushing the highest branches of the trees), the dark transparence of the water, the limpidity of the sun that a million leaves divided and vaporized into a floating mist like a sulphurous cloud, captured and glaucous—everything conspired in that abysmal aquarium of the air to fill Albert's soul with an eerie feeling that these were not the ordinary effects of light traversing our atmosphere but—and the thought made him shudder—that he was looking at an impossible *negative of the night*, and, as he lay at full length on the grassy bank, he leaned his face down close to the swift and vibratile surface of the water to touch its incalculable coolness with his cheeks. Great fishes were swimming in the transparent water, embellishing the depths with their lashing movements. A lurking life animated those depths above which all the terrestrial voices seemed to fall uniformly silent, instantly smothered by the rush of those violent cold waters pressing with an unendurable force against his eardrum, and sounding an inexorable alarm.

Once more his eye swept their calm surface and at once his brain recovered its lucidity. He had discovered the real *meaning* of this inconceivable landscape which he had until now only considered *upside-down*.

Out of the depth of that chasm, which stung his skin with its mortal chill, rose the trembling, watery visage of the sun, and the reflected colonnades of trees were ranged like heavy towers, lustrous and as smooth as copper, while under his eyes and lips, in the centre of this inverted peristyle of a solemn regularity, appeared the face of the sky like a merciful abyss, henceforth instantly opened, into which man might at last irrevocably plunge and satisfy without restraint what now to Albert was revealed as his most natural *inclination*.

For a second he closed his eyes under the charm and the terror and the intense pleasure of the temptation, and when he opened them again the curtain of trees was suddenly torn asunder beneath the water, and the reflected image of Herminien, walking without effort *under* the surface, came toward him through that forever forbidden world—and in the midst of the tumult of his terror and his ecstasy, which sent all the blood surging to his heart, could be heard distinctly the *ten strokes of a clock.*

Even the way Herminien was dressed, as he thus appeared to Albert in such an alarming fashion among the trees of the opposite bank, differed considerably from his usual attire. His head bare and his brown curls flying in the wind, he wore a long grey cloak that hung in austere folds from his shoulders and enveloped him completely. His face shone with a fraternal exaltation, and it seemed to Albert that this image out of the bottom of the river smiled at him with a smile whose calm and meditative fixity belonged to some region inaccessible to all human relationships. As though borne along by the web of an exalting music, his limbs seemed the prisoners of the fatal laws of a *number*—although a primary one in every respect—and his step majestic beyond all measure and at every moment plainly *oriented*, seemed to Albert the materialization, shorn for the first time of all kinds of grotesquely aesthetic veils, of what Kant has called, mysteriously enough, *purposiveness without purpose*. Whereas still governed by a quantity of the known laws of our planet, it seemed clear that his ways, perhaps for the first time, did not *exactly* coincide with the paths already traced, and that one could, without too great surprise, expect of this ambiguous apparition miracles, comparatively minor no doubt and not yet formally violating the physical laws already verified, but whose very ambiguity and air of derisive mystification could not fail to engender a feeling of uneasiness.

The curve of his two arms, raised in a gesture of ecstasy, suggested that of a lute, of which, it seemed strangely to Albert, Herminien was, at the same time, both the sound and the strings, and the landscape appeared to concentrate in him all its secret energy, to fire him with a supernatural and tremulous flame, and when he should open his *mouth*, one had every reason to expect to hear the powerful cry of the forest itself and of the mighty waters, for in a flash the bewitched mind accepted the idea that he occupied the very focal point, the precious and uniquely efficacious centre of this enormous and sonorous pavilion, and that he would shake the entire forest with the least breath of his voice. At that instant the curve of his arms was broken, he placed a finger on his lips, and with a gesture whose gentle seriousness seemed to caress the wall of the heart itself, he beckoned Albert to follow him.

Walking on opposite and parallel banks of the river with the rapid current between them, their reflections met in the very middle of the stream, smooth as a mirror. The shimmering freshness of the grass, the coolness of the air, the corollas of the big red flowers that bowed gracefully as they passed and seemed to distil a subtle and grave incense like the confident and devout soul of morning itself, gave to their silent peregrination the characters of a pilgrimage without a goal, and was for that very reason all the more perturbing. An extraordinary suspense filled Albert's soul, and his forehead, bent toward the ground, seemed to be bowed over his own plenitude. Around them the black depths of the forest seemed to grow denser with every step, the water, confined between its high banks, took on the flowing transparency of night. A rustic wooden bridge made of logs crudely put together, joined the two banks, and one behind the other they penetrated into the heart of the forest, and pressed forward among its precipitous gorges.

Soon, through the trunks of the trees covered with brilliant and elastic moss, through the branches twisted into fantastic arabesques, appeared the grey walls of a chapel overhanging the abyss. It presented the image of marvellous antiquity and in more than one place fragments of the delicate arches had fallen onto the black grass, where they shone like the white and scattered limbs of a hero treacherously felled, to whom the mysterious oratory would consecrate to the end of time the tears of an insatiable sorrow. Crazy vines with curiously lacy leaves, roots with vigorous thorns, and tufts of grey oats clung to the stones. On all sides the forest encircled it like a stifling cloak, and under the thick branches there floated a vague green twilight that had all the immobility of stagnant water: the place seemed so perfectly enclosed that the confined air could no more circulate there than in a long-closed room, and drifting around the walls in an opaque cloud, imbued for centuries with the persistent perfumes of moss and dried stones, it seemed like an odorant balm into which the precious relics had fallen. And yet, in the midst of this atmosphere of dream where time seemed miraculously suspended, an iron clock bristled with ominous arms, and the creaking, regular sound of its mechanism which it was impossible for the soul in the midst of these solitudes to connect in any way with the measurement of a time empty of all substance in these regions, and which seemed only the starting of some infernal machine, was immediately adopted by Albert as the explanation of the eerie sounds that had so terrified him on the banks of the river at the moment of Herminien's sudden apparition.

They entered the sanctuary through a low door. A heavy, dense air, a fragrant and almost total obscurity filled this refuge of prayer, in the middle of which, hanging from the vaulted ceiling, shone a lamp in a red globe whose marvellously fragile flame was constantly flaring up, bent over and lifted as by the beating of invisible wings. There were large breaches in the roof through which glided pell-mell, as into a deep abyss (and without the soul that was pierced to its very depths like the sharp point of a spear, being able to distinguish the sound of the light—the yellow and vibrant cry of the sun) the dazzling darts of the flaming breast of a bird. And the whole chapel, submerged in the green dusk diffused by its stained glass windows against which the leaves, indistinct through the dirt and thickness of the panes, floated with a movement more indolent and softer than seaweed, seemed to have *descended* into the gulfs of the forest as into some submarine grotto that pressed with all the force of its cool palms against these walls of glass and of stone, and to be held over these vertiginous depths only by the marvellous cable of the sun.

Their eyes, finally accustomed to the sudden obscurity, distinguished in one of the corners of the confined space, a large stone which was apparently the slab—as heavy as sleep—of an ancient tomb, and lingered for a few moments on the *ex voto* inscriptions in an ancient and almost indecipherable tongue, accompanying, it appeared, the offerings of a helmet and an iron lance which could be seen hanging on the darkest side of the deserted altar, and whose polished surfaces and sharp point, in spite of the persistent humidity of the walls, still preserved an astonishing brilliance. And a growing disquietude took hold of Albert's mind, deeply disturbed for many minutes now by these objects, whose character appeared so exclusively *emblematic*. It seemed to him that between the iron clock, the lamp, the tomb, the helmet and the lance there must be woven, perhaps through the effect of some ancient spell, but more likely because of their intimate and dangerous conjunction of an appalling antiquity, as the glistening saltpetre of the vault bore witness, a bond difficult in the circumstances to discover, but whose unquestionable existence imprisoned the imagination as in a perfect circle, and designated in an intentionally closed space the very geometric locus of the Enigma, whose inextricable knots had been stifling him since morning with an embrace at every instant more convincing—so that in the middle of his journey toward the altar he stopped abruptly, a prey to a sudden terror lest his enchanted footsteps, if they continued, should bring him face to face with its disconcerting and incontestable countenance.

Strange parallels, and not so much those of resemblance as those, in every respect more curious, of Analogy, all tending to imply that this visit, so altogether baffling, had not indeed been directed toward a chapel lost in the forest, but really toward some castle enchanted by the menace of the equivocal arms of the Fisher King, made a sudden ineffaceable inroad on his brain. The sun's rays shining down onto the middle of the empty and desolate altar, the sound of the heavy drops of water on the flagstones, the damp obscurity of the place, the song of the bird through the breach in the vault shriller than if it had burst inside the ear itself and as though fraught with an inexplicable and delirious hope, the regular ticking of the iron clock—all filled his soul with glorious and melancholy visions, exhausted it with an imperious and devastating suspense that rising, little by little, with the trills of the bird to a supreme point where it attained the consuming ardour of fire, in its vigorous plenitude wrung tears from the eyes no less than might the sound of the most sumptuous brass instruments. And perhaps it was not perceptible to him in the midst of his tumultuous agitation, how much higher than all the voices of nature resounded here with a dissonant clamour the glaring *disappropriation* of all things—of the altar all the more majestic for being abandoned, of the useless lance, of the tomb as perturbing as a cenotaph, of the clock *ticking for nothing* outside of time, on which its gears had no more grip than a mill-wheel in a dried-up stream, of the lamp burning in full daylight, of the windows palpably made to be looked *into* from *outside*, and against which were glued all the green tentacles of the forest.

Then out of the depth of his disquietude there rose a sound that seemed instantly to fill the whole chapel and stream down the glistening walls, and without daring to turn around, so stunned was he by its inconceivable amplitude, he now realized that during his own silent exploration of the chapel, Herminien had mounted the stone steps of the organ loft which rose in the darkness to the left of the door, occupying a considerable portion of the chapel, but which, his own attention having been at once captured by the alluring light effect, had escaped his notice until now. Herminien's playing was stamped with a singular force, and such was his expressive power that Albert, as though he could read in the depths of his soul, divined each succeeding theme of this wild improvisation. At first it seemed that Herminien, with dissonant and tentative gropings, interrupted by reiterations and regressions in which the principal motif was repeatedly taken up in a more timid and, as it were, interrogative mode, was only trying out the volume and acoustical capacity of this perturbing edifice. And now burst forth waves of sound, as violent as the forest and free as the winds of the heights, and the *storm* which Albert had contemplated with such horror from the high terraces of the castle thundered out of those mystic depths, while above them sounds of a crystalline purity fell, one by one, in a surprising and hesitating *decrescendo*, and floated like a sonorous vapour shot with flashes of yellow sunlight, curiously following the rhythm of the drops of water that were dripping from the vault.

After these effects of nature came an access of violent, sensual passion, and with perfect fidelity the organist painted his savage frenzy: like a luminous mist Heide floated on high, vanished, returned, and finally established her empire over melodic swells, of an extraordinary amplitude that seemed to transport the senses into an unknown region, and, by means of an incredible perversion, to endow the ear with all the graces of touch and sight. Meanwhile, although the artist had already given full rein to a tremulous and incoercible passion, it seemed to Albert apparent from now on, that even in the full plenitude of his improvisation, whose curious arabesques still kept something of the *tentative* character of an experiment, Herminien was searching for the key to an even loftier soaring, the necessary support for a final leap whose completely decisive consequences were at once both forecast and unpredictable, and that he was hesitating on the very brink of that abyss whose glorious approaches he described with such wild enveloping grace.

Clearly now—and with every moment it became more apparent to Albert—he was looking for the unique *angle of incidence* at which the eardrum, deprived of its power of interception and of diffusion, would become permeable like pure crystal, and would change this thing of flesh and blood into a sort of *prism of total reflection*, where sound would be accumulated instead of passing through, and would irrigate the heart with the same freedom as the sanguine medium, thus restoring to the desecrated word *ecstasy* its true significance. A sonorous vibration, growing ever more concentrated, seemed the exterior sign of the sombre fever of his quest, and settled everywhere *swarmingly* like bees out of a suddenly shattered hive. Finally a note, held with marvellous steadiness, shrilled in incredible splendour, and taking off as from a beach of sound, rose a phrase of ineffable beauty. And still higher, in a mellow golden light which seemed to accompany the descent into the chapel of a sublime grace as an answer to his prayer, Herminien's fingers resounded, as if a light and consuming warmth ran through them, the song of *virile fraternity*. And the final breath that gradually left the lungs as it soared to unbelievable heights, let the salutary tide of a sea, as light and free as the night, rise into the completely vacant body.

VII

THE FOREST

DURING THE DAYS that followed, endless rains descended upon Argol. Night and day, with unrelenting persistence, through all the echoing rooms could be heard the hammering of their myriad drops, and, in a slower rhythm, against the background of the shower that furiously lashed the ground, the fantastic dripping of the thick globules falling from the branches, one by one, like sterile, liquid fruit, and prolonging their measured strokes with the particular savagery, the inexplicable meticulousness of a torture. A heavy idleness took possession of the inmates of the castle, and with rare and insignificant words they appeared persistently to avoid each other, to such an extent that even their chance meetings in the mazes of the winding corridors, filled with a faltering white light which seeped through the curtains of the rain as though diffused by the moisture ceaselessly streaming down the walls, engendered a visible malaise. Even their protracted and assiduous meditations borrowed from the hypnotic monotony of the rain a strange and persistent perspicacity that passed into and continued without any apparent diminution through their dreams even in the midst of their quiet slumber, which now, in the heart of the dim twilight reigning throughout the castle, had become their most natural and, without restriction, their fullest mode of existence—and from which each morning they were awakened not so much by the imperfect daylight as by a gradual and singular *clairvoyance*.

And so, in the midst of an indefinable anxiety in which the lucid conscience scrutinized, one by one, the most secret recesses of the heart, unfolded another wholly imaginary day which, throughout its entire lugubrious duration, wore the blank, wan look attributed in most descriptions to the dawn. It seemed as though the different scattered members of the day, unable to reassemble so far from the heat of the sun, wandered desperately under the grey cope of the sky, and, here and there, one could see in their own hideous shred of light, as in the faint light of a beacon, the icy glint of the waters of a spring, the greyish mud of an inexplicable path that could only lead to the horrible and vacuous waste-countries of the rain.

It now seemed ever more certain to Albert that the improvisation which Herminien had given voice to in the chapel and whose echoes kept ceaselessly resounding in his memory, had less the value of a caprice of his sensibility troubled by that strange pilgrimage, than of an act and an appeal—and that Herminien had sought in the soothing balm of music, not so much an appeasement of his sufferings, as a protection against an ineluctable temptation. Albert found in his own heart the proof that interests other than those of a passing and purely aesthetic emotion had been weighing in the balance, when he remembered the anxiety which had gripped it in the chapel, that anxiety whose indefinite nature, whose surprising character of a *warning*, could only be ascribed to some precarious struggle in which the forces of life and death themselves were at stake. And so it was that when the deathly rays of the sun reappeared, throwing wide open for them the forest's snares once more, he had the overwhelming feeling that the *days of the end* were now at hand.

On an afternoon of crushing heat which seemed by its intensity to bleach all the blue out of the sky, as colour from some airy fabric, Albert sat in the tower room overlooking the high terraces. He gazed at the woods of Storrvan, at all that austere landscape, and suddenly it seemed to him that the sea of trees flowing without a break to the horizon was completely detached from the world, separated by the malediction of a magic spell, and that it had begun to turn around the castle like a wheel whose movement nothing could stop, and as terrifying as the apparently slow motion, inappreciable and as it were *secondary*, of the blades of a propeller turning at its very maximum speed. And, in truth, he was convinced that this world surrounding him was sustained in its ghostly fixity only by the tension, now approaching its limit, of some unimaginable force that, by a miracle, kept it from dissolution, and that all these fragile phenomena whose very passivity constituted the real terror for the soul, must perforce be shattered and fly to pieces before his eyes at the slightest loss of speed.

In the midst of this frenzy which his reason could only with difficulty control, he glanced down and saw Herminien and Heide leave the castle and disappear into the forest. Their erect shadows ran rapidly along the ground, and Albert's eye caught sight of the long barrel of a rifle slung over Herminien's shoulder, which he followed for a long time as it glinted cruelly through the curtain of forest trees, appearing and disappearing at intervals with the unendurable gleam of a naked sword.

Little by little, Albert slipped into a profound reverie in which the flash of that hostile steel in the midst of exhausting and equivocal meditations, seemed to reappear at long intervals like those luminous streaks left on the retina by a too dazzling light, emerging finally as a dominant motif and, in the midst of dim and indistinct images, invariably accompanied by an indefinable sensation of an impending *danger*. And below this obsessive recurrence, deep in his memory, some obscure travail seemed to be going on, without his mind, prostrate and totally inert, lending the least participation. In the mass of his memories, slight and almost molecular detachments and displacements seemed to be taking place under the pressure of a prodigious weight, and, like iron filings moved by an invisible magnet on a piece of paper, seemed to shape themselves, did finally shape themselves, into what now appeared to be an interpretable *figure*, but which his feverish reason, struck with a furious impotence, *circled* without success, and as though under a spell, recognized the clearly oriented lines without yet, by intuition, penetrating their suddenly dazzling significance. Then the lines seemed once more to blur like those of a landscape reflected in water, and at the moment when the mind, a prey to the most harrowing despair, was being buffeted furiously on the waves, brusquely one single feature floated up from the wreck, unimaginably descriptive and familiar, and a fiery hand began to fashion the secret capacity of the soul as though into a perfect mould to which the face of truth itself adhered, too narrowly and too near to be then decipherable.

For a long time these exhausting efforts continued, and when at last Albert's eyes, until now turned inward through the effect of intense concentration, looked out over the landscape again and for a moment rested there, he was filled with an unendurable sensation of *solitude*. Coming out of his quest among equivocal phantoms of the past, a quest equalling in its distracting power that of sleep itself, it suddenly seemed to him that it had been many long mortal hours since Herminien and Heide had left the castle, and this sudden blank in his consciousness seemed to confer on this time left behind, this lost time, an unparalleled value. In the midst of a growing anxiety, in a paralyzing suspense, he strode through the rooms and out onto the terraces, vainly questioning the horizon which over its whole extent preserved a merciless immobility. Great storm clouds bore down slowly on the forest, and the approach of dusk, which gave an *objective* and now undeniable strangeness to the prolonged absence of the castle guests, redoubled his nervous tension. Lowering his worried gaze to the inner courts of the castle he saw, lying asleep on the stones in a pose of torpid prostration, the same servant who had met him on the day of his arrival. And this disconcerting sight sent a chill through his heart, as though his glance—for it was apparent that the man was plunged into the heart of a purely animal realm, and to such a degree that it would have seemed scarcely surprising, as one realized with a sickening shudder, to see, when he awoke, the face of a leopard turned toward the sky, instead of that of a man—had borne the mark of an exorbitant and sacrilegious *indiscretion*.

Large drops began to fall hesitatingly, resounding on the leaves, then stopped, and this rain, powerless to cool, suddenly made tangible the stifling density of the heat. And the threat of storm everywhere present in the painful immobility of the air, in the fuliginous hue of the sky, and in the anguish that filled the body and drove the soul to the very frontiers of madness, was far crueller than its imminent outburst.

Down the empty and echoing stairs, through the deserted courtyards, Albert fled the castle and plunged into the funereal solitudes of the forest. The horror of those lonely woods was deepened by the approach of night. At this troubling hour of twilight, it seemed that everywhere—in the crackings of the over-heated bark, in the strangely reverberating fall of a dead branch in a deserted avenue, in the mist floating around the dense masses of the trees, in the intermittent cries of a belated bird flying lazily from branch to branch like a fortuitous guide—a redoubtable alchemy was at work behind impenetrable veils as the forest prepared its nocturnal mysteries.

Soon Albert lost himself in the circuitous windings of the woods. Little by little, as the majesty and silence of the trees unconsciously took possession of him, his pace grew slower and finally, his body filled with a painful weariness, he sank down on the moss, and stretched out at full length beside a murmuring spring whose pure waters flowed among the roots of a gigantic pine. Above his head the bright colours faded in the sky and the first stars shone sweetly between the motionless branches. Finally, the moon rose, enormous and round, behind the trunk of the pine and suddenly it seemed to be hanging on the pine's branches, very bright and near, like an enormous shield not a stone's throw away. The continuous and monotonous noise of the brook so close to his head gradually filled him with a flow of sweetness, which laid over him in a transparent bath of calm oblivion, and seemed, in its timid insistence, to triumph even over the tumult of his blood, assuaged now in the coolness of the night. Freed from the furious pounding of his heart, he was now astonished by the delicate accuracy of awareness and the power of suggestion his senses had acquired: from of the intoxicating odour of the resin of the pines, the silvery quivering of the leaves, the velvet darkness of the sky, with every second, he was born into a new life which reflected the same intensity as the incredible vigour of his perceptions. Silently, in limpid peace, his spirit rose toward the branches softly lighted by the moon, lost itself in the purifying freshness of the night, and such became the exclusive power of attention of his captivated hearing, that the noise of the brook seemed gradually to swell over its stony bed and, risen to the proportions of a tumultuous roar, to fill the entire forest with its crystalline harmonies, and even to transform into sounds of an ineffable transparency the pools of silver which fell from the moon.

However, as the night advanced and the chill of the damp air, imprisoned by the branches along the ground, became more penetrating, the melting power, the witchery of the night seemed to wane; and as his head turned slightly, suddenly his eyes closed again and his arms crossed themselves over his heart as though to protect it from the approach of some invisible terror. Among the long tufts of grass floating in the waters of the spring near his head, it seemed to him that, in a flash, there had been stamped on the retina of his eye, *one* tuft ineffably different from all the others, whose undulating movement and particularly fine silky substance made it *impossible for him to be mistaken*. In his despair, he kept his eyes closed for a long time, seeking in vain to flee into the depth of an abyss of darkness and oblivion, while he pressed his hands tightly over the appalling leaping of his heart. But *already he knew*. With a bound he was on his feet, was gazing down at Heide's completely naked body. Her hair was floating in long swirls over the water and her head, thrown back and lost in the shadows where only her bare teeth shone, was raised at an appalling angle to her body, lifting toward the sky her round breasts caressed by the unbearable ardours of the moon. Blood, like the petals of a living flower, stained and bespattered her belly and open thighs, darker than the rivers of the night, more fascinating than its stars, and around her wrists, tied together behind her back, a thin rope had penetrated the flesh and disappeared completely under a tiny red line from which a drop of blood oozed with an insane deliberateness, rolled down one finger, and fell into the water of the spring with a curiously musical sound.

VIII

THE AVENUE

ONCE MORE grey vapours covered the sky, and the castle seemed to be buried under an avalanche, a continual crashing of cold waters. For Heide and Albert, after the flash of catastrophe, it seemed that slowly, slowly their life there began again with all the intoxicating relish of convalescence. Herminien had disappeared from the castle and no one knew what had become of him.

Long days went by, and a visible change seemed to take place in Albert. New forces awoke in him like the sudden rising of sap, like the pushing up of new life. Once more he took deep draughts of the invigorating forest air. Fresh vigour glided through his muscles. All day long he gave himself up to the most exhausting exertions; sometimes bringing a wild boar of the woods to bay, and as though dazed by the proximity of danger, feeling in the midst of an unforgettable spasm, the sharp tusks of the cornered beast grazing his belly, sometimes exhausting his horse in endless rides along the edge of the ocean, torn to its depths by the fierceness of the storm. Often, unable to contain the life bursting in his breast, leaving his horse to stretch its lean neck toward the yellow and salty grasses, whinnying fearfully at the furious gusts of wind, Albert would throw himself into the roaring sea, cleaving the waves with a heart full of anger, and then thrown back at last onto the shore, and conscious only of the hot pounding of his blood behind his closed eyelids, he seemed to feel, still bearing down upon his shoulders, up on his palms now pressed against the sand, the weight of the whole ocean that was yet unable to cool the burning ardour of the illimitable desires to which he had not yet given a name. It seemed to him that within the sweep of his wide arms, within the boundless gulf of his heart, with its powerful appetites, he could contain the entire earth. Then streaming with water and his skin drinking in the icy shower through all its pores as though trying to draw its divine coldness into his heart, he would plunge into the muddy dominion of the rain, into the depth of the forest devastated and swept like a beach by the transparent wind.

Sometimes his thoughts took a different course. It would seem to him that he had tasted some forbidden fruit of the tree of life with sharp thorns, and that he still felt its savour against his teeth—and he felt that over and above the bitter gift of knowledge which he had so often called on out of the depths of the disquietude of his heart, into it had descended with all its poisonous juices, the mysterious gifts of *sympathy*. That he had tasted of the blood of the dragon, and understood the language of birds. Then a veil of blood across his eyes, a quivering of his lips would announce the disconcerting approach of the atrocious and ineffable *object*. And lying at full length in the wet grass which he would gnaw in a transport of rage, his face streaming with his own salt tears, he would evoke the white vision of Heide in the bottomless pit of that night of which nothing could ever equal the horror and the fascination. He saw her shackled limbs as though melted and reassembled by the crushing majesty of the thunderbolt, her whole body more ravished, pierced, branded, palpitating, bruised, mangled and lacerated than by the nine swords, streaming with blood, burning with a rosy fire, of a blinding and unendurable radiance, all the marvellous substance of her flesh spurting out like a fruit in the sharp talons of destiny. And this white corpse with the wounds of the thunderbolt, the head thrown back, eyes lost in a mournful spell, took him in a backward course on a static, rocking voyage.

Then, his eyes closed, his temples throbbing in a consuming anguish, he felt the wound of her belly come to him. It inundated his eyelids with the savage, savage and blinding, baptism of her blood, and, line by line with fearful tension, weary of the pursuit of the glorious mysteries of the world, he followed the path of a drop of blood along a finger. And now the life of his soul seemed attached to that absurd drop, and he felt that all he had loved, all that he had sought flowed with that sombre drop to the bottom of the spring. And with eyes closed, he glued his lips to that red fountain and, drop by drop, he let the mysterious, the delicious blood stream over his lips. Like a sharp thorn he plunged this vision into the depth of his heart which it pierced better than the red fire of a lance, felt blissfully its adorable sting, while a merciless trembling scourged all his living flesh, and he felt himself melting in an extenuating compassion. And now let him confront his fate and an end which was hardly doubtful any longer, let him confront fate that had not turned him into a pillar of salt, he whose eyes had looked upon what they *should not have seen.*

He dared not admit to himself that he was thinking of Herminien, and doubtlessly also some recollection of Catholic dogma, while seeming to justify and increase his power of concentration on the place of Heide's stigmata which, prevented him, on the other hand, from considering with more than a purely conventional shame the one who now appeared to him as the black angel of the Fall and its dangerous herald. And yet, beyond the pitiful distinctions of good and evil, his mind through an avenging dialectic, embraced Herminien in fraternal connivance. Whatever the transport of hate, whatever the degree of horror that scene might have encompassed, far beyond hate and horror Heide and Herminien must henceforth exist together, sealed to each other in all the lightning glare of the incomparable Event. Together till the end of time, inseparable accomplices like the victim and the knife, united and justified in the fecundity of their miracle, in the light of the unique instantaneous *image* they had created. For him too, as for Heide, Herminien would be the living salt of his wound, the food of his torturing disquietude. Wherever they went, there he would be, dragging himself at the feet of this couple of marble with vacant bluish eyes, more troubling than a statue dug up in a garden, more perverting than a time-machine, more demoralizing than the undiscoverable *rock of offence*. Yes, tinged with the overwhelming magic of her blood, his face bent over her face upside down, which before his eyes, as silent as oil, was beginning its incessant journey backward, Herminien was joined to her more closely than on a baleful pack of cards, through the incredible contempt of the artist, like a monstrous trump card, the bust of the king of spades to that of the queen of hearts.

Lying at full length on the mass of furs, her feet bare, her hair dishevelled, a dark cloak around her shoulders, Heide shielded herself from the painful attacks of the daylight, her benumbed mind seeking refuge in an eternal twilight. She had come out of that night of terror as out of the buoyant depths of cold waters, inert, empty, broken, sweetly worn out. Without hate, without anger, mortally crushed, she still felt Herminien's power upon her like the salty fortifying deluge of the living waters of the sea whose mysterious waves without shock or effort swiftly bore her along on a voyage without return, to deposit her on the *other shore* of the ocean whose solemn and overwhelming expanse she explored with the graces of a child's groping fingers, and as though restored to her primitive virginity. It seemed to her that she was ceaselessly wandering and coming to rest on the buoyant waves of a body floating like hair, spread over the world like a carpet of felicity. Her last resistance had given way deep within her, and everything was light—light, loosened, detached, floating, iridescent, unreal, entangled like the threads of a skein of silk in the wind, in the depths of the darkness of that room where she lay motionless, surrounded by her aerial body, floating, flying, unreal as the clouds of the sky and like them forever chased by the great wind.

And it seemed to her that she now lived in Albert as his chosen child, bathed in the very dawn of the world, in the shimmering glow of limbo. Out of the depths of that night now hidden from her by the sudden cataract of great waters, out of her annihilation, little by little, she was reborn in him. Again she saw how he came toward her in the moonlight, with the calm of his eyes, the inexplicable simplicity of his gestures as though immersed once more in original purity, and how he bathed her, kissed and clothed her, and his arms around her, supported her, and how she felt more deliciously encompassed than by a legion of angels from heaven, felt something more inundating and sweeter than *consciousness in sleep* would be, confiding herself to him forever in delirious trust, in an absolute abandonment of herself above an abyss in which henceforth only his arms could bury her. Stripped of her annihilated body, of her numbed senses, floating over the forest like a soul ready to be taken, as unarmed and unattached as the Walkyrie, *his* mouth then gave her breath, *his* hand brought a hand to life, and in an unbelievable kiss of the soul, it seemed to her that by Albert she had been *disembodied* forever.

Soon began the glorious days of autumn particularly unmistakable in the melancholy curve that the sun, already noticeably lower over the horizon, drew across the sky, in whose calm expanses as though constantly swept by a wonderfully pure wind, its golden trace seemed to linger like the wake of a magnificent ship, and hardly had it turned its course toward the horizon than the moon, as though attached to the beam of a celestial balance, appeared against the blue light of day with the ghostly glow of an unexpected star, whose malignant influence would now, of itself alone, explain the sudden, strange, and half-metallic alterations of the leaves of the forest whose surprising red and yellow brilliance burst out everywhere with the irrepressible vigour, the fulminating contagion of a luxuriant leprosy of the vegetable kingdom. In this calm atmosphere the castle was filled with light echoing noises, and often Heide and Albert, seized with an inexplicable uneasiness, would find themselves together in the great drawing-room, to which they seemed drawn by the expectation of the arrival of some disturbing visitor—and as their eyes met, an embarrassment was born between them that grew more painful with each succeeding second.

Heide's already extraordinary pallor visibly increased with each day of this pale, cold season, with the ever shorter appearances of the heatless sun, from which her face seemed, and in a way that now appeared fatal to Albert with the decline of autumn, to draw all its luminous life. And the constant *fading* of that angelic countenance, as though afflicted by the same malady that was ravaging the trees of the forest, startled Albert, and plunged him into an inexhaustible and disquieting reverie. They would then engage in vague and languishing conversations whose mingling sound would more and more frequently dwindle into a stifled vibration still perceptible for a long time in the silence that seemed to close around them with a curiously engulfing power, and again would begin what they dared not admit without terror was nothing but an interminable *waiting*. Then their eyes, with un-erring instinct, would turn toward the tall French windows behind which the dancing shadows of the branches, constantly outlined in a slow and gentle swaying, revealed the oppressive presence of the forest. And the whole drawing-room in the declining day was filled with the shadow of the branches, with their dark abundance, which plunged them into the heart of the forest in a silence that no longer protected them from its encroaching arms, and the brilliant, yellow splashes of sunlight, gliding through the stained glass onto the walls, seemed to their bewitched eyes to indicate not the steadily advancing hour of the day, but, on the contrary, like a precise *level*, to mark the overwhelming oscillations of the entire mass of the castle struggling like a ship in distress on the powerful swells of the forest.

Then sometimes, in a gust of wind, the doors of one of the tall windows would open with a symmetrical solemnity and while their blood rushed suddenly to their hearts, and the long draperies one after the other rose and swelled with eerie slowness in the midst of the wild and suddenly magnified noise of the wind, great volleys of dried leaves would whirl through the lofty room with an icy whirring, and the shivering skeletons of the leaves' dried veins would alight on furniture and carpet with the dislocated jerks of exhausted birds. And, looking away from each other, they dared not, in the terror of their hearts, measure the intensity of their desperate and deceived expectation by the tragic shock which had made both of them leap up at the first sound. And the wind, with the mysterious deliberateness of a hand, unrolled one by one the heavy folds of the silken curtains slowly swelling and unfurling like sails; but the mass of those dark fabrics had long since resumed their severe rigidity when, at the farthest end of the room lost in semi-darkness, a vast brown hanging, with a great slapping sound in the midst of the completely restored silence, seemed in the inexplicable heaving of its ample folds, like the image of a convulsion, as weirdly autonomous as a face rising out of the darkness and suddenly touched by concentric waves of terror.

However, their fear was dissipated in the resplendent light of day. The amazing radiance which every morning rose from the clear surface of the river drew them lingeringly through the light mist still veiling the high branches of the trees, and, falling on them in fine drops, seemed by the evidence of their wet faces the true mark of the *baptism* of the new day, the refreshing and delectable anointment of the morning. Little by little, the trees came confusedly out of the mist and as though by a unique privilege, stripped of their particularly picturesque quality, filled the barely awakened soul with the pure consciousness of their *volume* and of their harmonious luxuriance in the heart of a landscape in which colour seemed to lose completely its ordinary power of localization and, on the shores of these calm waters, inscribed for the eye, freed as by a miracle from all that the ordinary work of perception contains of a *reductio ad absurdum*, appeared only the soothing and almost divine conjunction of the horizontal plane and the sphere. And nature, restored by the fog to its secret geometry, now became as unfamiliar as the furniture of a drawing-room under dust-covers to the eye of an intruder, substituting, all at once, the menacing affirmation of pure volume for the familiar hideousness of utility, and by an operation whose magical character must be evident to any one, restoring to the instruments of humblest use, until then dishonoured by all that *handling* engenders of base degradation, the particular and striking splendour of the *object*.

With slow steps, they entered the forest, virgin in every respect, and pursued their way along those noble avenues. And now the sun showed above the crests of the high mountains, a cool breeze swayed the trees, and the roughened waters sparkled with a thousand lights, but all day long the bluish shadow of an iridescent fog still lingered over the horizon as though kept at a distance only by the radiation of this luminous couple. Unbelievable then was their felicity, their inexhaustible and absorbing bliss, and into the deep waters of each other's eyes, into their depths, they plunged like strong swimmers, and prolonged to the point of dizziness the fixity of their intolerable gaze, in which alternated the very ice of the abysses and the atrocious fires of the sun. They could not satisfy their inexorable eyes, devastating suns of their hearts, dripping suns, suns of the sea, suns sprung drenched from the lowest depths, icy and trembling like a living jelly in which light has been made flesh by the operation of an inconceivable spell.

One day, through the trees, they followed a wide green avenue covered by a vaulting of branches a hundred feet overhead, whose singular character, immediately apparent to the soul always on the alert for the perpetual snares of the forest, was due to the fact that while it ran through particularly hilly country and continually embraced each slightest sinuosity, yet the *rigidity* of its direction imposed itself upon the eye in the midst of all the natural undulations of the ground, and, directly in front of the traveller through the dark barrier of trees at the horizon, carved a luminous and sharply defined notch—suggesting to the mind, obsessed by the impenetrable wall of trees, a door opening onto an entirely unknown country which, because of the insistent straightness of the avenue drawn over hill and dale as by some wild caprice, by a will royally disdainful of all difficulties, seemed to confer a gift of supreme attraction. Amazing, too, was the indubitable *exaggeration* of its dimensions, leaving between the glorious walls of lofty verdure the span of a veritable clearing covered with a carpet of grass, vast and empty as the bare stage of a theatre, and whose colossal width seemed destined to reveal gradually to the soul all the, by no means ordinary, terrors of *agoraphobia*. And yet, in spite of the abnormal urgency suggested by the straightness of this cut—as though on a planet inhabited by mad geometers it had been considered of prime necessity to paint *first of all* the meridians on the ground—the character of pure *direction*, free from all idea of a goal, seemed in its peremptory affirmation alone sufficient —Albert and Heide turning to look back, noticed, not without a feeling of uneasiness, that the avenue only a short distance behind them, gradually invaded by the extravagant vegetation of the underbrush, little by little relinquished its geometric majesty and was lost in the *impasse* of the uniform ocean of trees.

Nothing can convey an idea of the suggestive power of this *road*, open for the soul alone in the heart of a forest isolated from the world, and which, by the disconcerting amplitude of its useless dimensions, seemed to render more complete the solitude of these sequestered regions. At this moment the sun, low in its course, shone in the very middle of the trench, which the avenue cut through the trees all the way to the distant horizon, and filled the theatrical vessel with a flood of golden light: as far as the eye could see the double colonnade of trees, more motionless than a curtain of leaves reflected in a sheet of water, seemed to make way before it; and, as on a path opened through the sea, and in the midst of a silence more sumptuous than that of an empty palace and which seemed to hold all things in suspense in the sustained flash of its enchantment, Heide and Albert started down the middle of the avenue. For a long time through the declining hours of the day, they followed the implacable rigidity of the route, colliding with the suffocating walls of their destiny.

Sometimes a bird flew like a triumphant arrow across the avenue, and its particular and now surprising *immunity*, during its whole passage across what seemed, even to the least initiated eye, one of the authentic *high-tension lines* of the globe, had an effect on the mind akin to watching the nerve-racking gymnastics of a sparrow on an electric wire. Sometimes a brook crossed the path, recognized far off by the singular gaiety, the entirely gratuitous musicality of the murmur of its transparent waters, and Albert then with a fraternal grace, would take Heide's shoes from her tired feet, improvising a scene comparable, by the excessive force of its effect upon the soul abandoned in these lonely haunts, with that scene which the critic of symphonies has designated by a completely strange title—because it suggests, and intends to suggest, that certain human relations lost in an animality as pure and fluent as thought, are completely reducible to an element for the first time envisaged *from within*—of "scene beside the brook".

At last night fell over the forest and the sky revealed all its stars, but nothing could stop their divine course, guarded more surely within the temple in the woods than by the tutelary sphinxes along the avenues of the Egyptian tombs. *Trust*, restored Albert and Heide to the state of pure virtue and resembling the milky emanation of the night bathed by the moon, visited them with all its primitive grace. As once before, on that harrowing day, across the watery plains of the sea, retreat was now no longer possible. But the night

115

lingered and the avenue stretched out in all its fatal length. And they knew now that their road would end only with the surprising splendour of the morning. And this couple, arms linked over shoulders, endlessly prolonged their enchanted walk with eyes closed, hair flying, bare feet on moss out of the strange tales of chivalry, and with their slightest gestures visibly surrounded by all the signs of a *false elegance* a thousand times more disturbing than the real.

Long lingered the hours of the profound night. And now a vague feeling they were powerless to resist invaded the souls of Heide and of Albert. It seemed to them that the planet, swept along by the heart of the night which it belaboured with the crests of all its trees, overturned and spun backward following the obstinate direction of the avenue, more unreal than the axis of the poles, more abundant than the sun's rays drawn in chalk on a blackboard. And as though lifted by a prodigious effort onto the roof of the smooth planet, onto the nocturnal ridge of the world, they felt, with a divine shudder of cold, the sun sinking under them to an immense depth, and the unballasted avenue as it climbed right through the thickness of the true night revealing to them, minute by minute, all its secret and untrodden paths. In the silence of the woods, hardly distinguishable from that of the stars, they lived through a night of the world in all its sidereal intimacy, and the revolution of the planet, its thrilling orb, seemed to govern the harmony of their most ordinary gestures.

Now, however, it appeared to them that they were crossing low and watchful plains, interspersed with stagnant waters, where reeds like spears rose in supernatural immobility, then the road slowly climbed an imposing hill where a lighter air presaged still incommensurable altitudes—and often they would look back avidly, trying to make out the levelled landscape still completely covered by the dense veils of night. But their mad anguish was drawing to an end. A gentle breeze out of the black sky swayed the funereal folds of what seemed at first the unknown and unnameable substance of primeval chaos itself, but that finally proved to be only a heavy covering of grey clouds hovering over this nightmare landscape. And morning with its wings swept the shivering stretches of pure solitude. And, as though at the brusque signal of a warning gun, Heide and Albert stood still.

The gigantic avenue ended at the very summit of the plateau. In the middle of a level heath swept at this moment by the morning breeze, stretched a vast circular arena, appearing and disappearing in the capricious vagaries of the trailing mist, and very exactly delimited by a tender and luminous grassy turf which rendered its circumference clearly discernible, and contrasted strangely with the dishevelled, brambly and in every way utterly lugubrious character of the bushes carpeting the hillside. Cordons of stones scattered negligently here and there, which owed to the growth of the lichen now cloaking them their eerie hue of long bleached bones, accentuated for the eye the exorbitant circumference, and redoubled an almost intolerable perplexity. For, avenues in every respect *exactly similar* to the one Heide and Albert had been following here converged from all parts of the horizon, and from this vantage point the eye could encompass the entire vast perspective. It would be difficult for me to make the reader fully understand the impression produced upon Heide and Albert by this very strictly *incongruous* manifestation of the combined efforts of nature and art, unless it is realized that the most conclusive motive for the oppression transmitted to their minds from all sides, was that of an irrevocable and yet incomprehensible *necessity*. And perhaps the word *rendezvous* with the double meaning it implies—by a twist, whose profound cruelty is here apparent—of carefully concerted machinations and, at the same time, of the entire abdication of all the purely defensive reflexes, would best translate the dismayed impression instantly produced on the spectators of the scene by the perverse uselessness of this grandiose décor.

Meantime, while they wandered lost in the last

shreds of shadow still lingering over these uplands, the pounding of a runaway horse's hoofs could be heard, and soon the animal appeared filling the deserted plateau with the noise of its furious galloping, its body covered with foam which it tossed wildly around it on every side, while on its back—and apparently the very centre of those convulsions which at moments started it frantically plunging—could be seen an empty saddle. Then they both recognized—and with a shudder of sudden anguish identified by *that empty saddle*—Herminien's favourite horse.

Fallen in the grass, coiled in the grass, more motionless than a meteoric stone, with the strange floating uncertainty of his wide-open corpse's eyes, as though revived in his face after death by the secret hand, and with the disquieting insinuations of an embalmer, the eyelids seemingly touched by the majestic make-up of death, Herminien lay nearby, and his uncovered face in the icy nakedness of the morning radiated a silent horror, as though, through the effect of a bloody irony, the blackness of a crime accomplished without a witness were painted on the face of the victim himself. Near him a block of sandstone half hidden in the grass was the very one on which his horse's hoof must have stumbled.

Silently they lifted him, removed his clothes, and his torso appeared, white, vigorous and soft—and their eyes obstinately avoided each other—and in his side below his ribs, appeared the hideous wound where the horse's shoe had struck, black and bloody, circled with clotted blood as though the haemorrhage had been stopped only by the effect of a charm or of a philtre. Little by little, they felt life returning under their fingers and it was not long before the doors of the castle closed behind the wounded man in a silence full of foreboding. And all during the grey and ghostly day, filled with the ṣame magic as the night, while the sun's white disc remained obstinately hidden behind heavy mists, Albert continued to wander through the long empty corridors lighted, as though by the eerie reflections of the snow, by the continuously diffused light of the white sky, soft, and with a look of blindness, a prey to an intense agitation comparable only to the highest state of tension of one who keeps vigil. And whenever he passed in front of the closed door of Herminien's room, behind which the timid clink of a glass, and the musical and surprising sound of an isolated sigh in the heart of the tense silence acquired the majestic and uncertain accents of life and death themselves, all the blood in his veins would leap up in a fiery surge.

Worn out with fatigue, he at last lay down outside that forbidden door, and was soon visited by funereal visions. His dream seemed to take him back to those far-off days when, with Herminien on calm summer nights, their intoxicating walks would take them all over sleeping Paris, revealing to them, in the midst of a conversation inordinately interrupted by silence and invariably leading them by capricious roundabout ways to the vicinity of the jardin du Luxembourg, mysteriously deserted at that hour, the splendour of the nocturnal leaves, more entrancing than a stage setting in the light of the street lamps. And now, for the last few moments, their ears, no longer heeding their own desultory words, seemed to distinguish besides the hypnotic hissing of the arc lights, a similar and surprisingly moving noise coming from behind the high black walls cutting off their view on all sides, which was, it soon became evident, the collective murmuring of a kneeling invisible crowd praying in the middle of the street in a perfect delirium of unrestrained fervour. And now they found themselves drawn by these sounds into the maze of narrow and perpetually deserted streets that connect the place Saint-Sulpice with the rue de Vaugirard.

Little by little, the noise of the voices seemed to fill the sky like a fiery red illumination, and the rumbling roar of those multitudinous voices in the midst of the starry night, together with the endless humming of the arc lights, ended by completely bewildering them. And at the same moment they knew, and knew, both of them, that they knew: it was for the soul of

Herminien, Herminien, *condemned to death*, that this crowd was praying, and its verdict was accepted by both of them at the same instant with an air of heroic and indifferent *resolution*. A few steps farther on they entered the vestibule of a dark house, and saw straight ahead of them (*communicating* apparently with the street through the intermediary of a particular phenomenon which consisted in this: that as the noise of the prayers diminished in the street a similar murmur of voices grew proportionately louder but whose character was nevertheless indefinably *interior*) what appeared to be—because of the huge blackboard, the childish scrawlings in chalk, the shiny aspect and tiny dimensions of the tables and benches with which it was furnished—a simple school room. Judges were sitting on a long low platform and through the open door could be heard the confused hum of their voices chanting in unison with curious emphasis.

At the same time, in the midst of a scattered audience, filling the benches in semi-darkness, whose empty faces seemed to him to reflect only the particularly tedious reading of the verdict, Albert through a mass of backs silhouetted against the light and cutting curiously across his horizon, was finally able to examine the ominous instrument of death, which appeared to consist of two long wooden bars *moving freely* in space in front of the blackboard, as though before this surface, now grown magical, the enigmatic play of *two straight lines in space* (which the impotent hand of the schoolmaster had so often tried to summon to the heart of a space, real at last) had leapt into an existence whose very crudeness, whose curious air of imperfection, seemed to constitute the seal of their terrible reality—and had finally begun, on their own account, the malefic and disquieting orgy of their unpredictable movements. Then Herminien took his place on the platform in front of the blackboard and instantly became the room's living centre of attention. At first it seemed that the long wooden bars, nimbler than knitting needles, were executing all around him an interminable and graceful dance, in which the play of constantly variable angles in itself constituted for him a profound intellectual *diversion*, then the tempo was accelerated, and, like the sharp plunges of a maddened beast, they improvised flourishes more harrowing than a dance of swords.

Soon, however, in a movement become suddenly calm, with a curious and excessive slowness, now for the first time the bars seemed to have a tendency to become *parallels*, approaching each other in a henceforth inexorable movement, giving to this intoxicating exercise the indefinable glitter, the suddenly jerky and feverish movements of a dance of death, for

Herminien's neck was now caught between the bars, and the whole audience, becoming aware of this at the same instant, fastened upon it with one accord their passionate attention. For everyone it became evident from now on that the two bars, whose abstract character of purely geometric *straight lines* had never been lost sight of in the course of this dance of magic rods, and was now felt to constitute all the veritable horror, engaged as they were in this parallel move-ment seeming to have no other object than to become absorbed in each other, to return to their primitive unity. And then, in the midst of the tense silence, could be heard the unmistakable noise of cartilages cracking under a pressure which was already beyond endurance. Meanwhile, on Herminien's face, impas-sive up to the moment, just as the first fissure in a building through its very *insignificance* seems to con-tain in its fatal and still imperceptible beginning all the overwhelming horror of an earthquake, a first imperceptible wrinkle at the corner of his lips seemed now the sign of an atrocious and startling alteration of the features—and on the very threshold of mad-ness a pious hand turned Albert's head away, and standing beside him he then recognized (aware of her presence by the fact that she alone, at the same moment, also turned her head away)—Heide.

IX

THE ROOM

MEANWHILE, HERMINIEN came slowly out of the shadow of death, and soon his still faltering footsteps could be heard echoing through the mournful labyrinths of the castle which Heide now obstinately shunned—and began a slow convalescence whose final issue was still rendered uncertain by his persistent and abnormal pallor. A poignant feeling of mystery now kept drawing Albert toward his room, where the shutters were always closed, and which seemed sanctified by the enigma of his resurrection—and he would stay there gazing at the mysterious door, lingering outside the threshold with a mad smile on his lips. But it became more and more difficult for him to *wait*, the desire that possessed him having long since passed the limits of ordinary curiosity. He was obsessed by the idea, which grew stronger day by day, that the room, bewitched by that hidden and now intensely dramatic presence, would perhaps reveal the *secret* which he had never ceased—he admitted it now in the fever of danger—to seek during the whole course of this friendship, so long, so dubious and so treacherous, that he had formed with Herminien. Forever before his eyes, and as in a semi-delirium, stretched the inviolable, nocturnal avenue, and it seemed to him in the light of the recollection of that night, that even the most notoriously insignificant events of his life—and along practically uncharted paths—had oriented him toward the one who held in his hands the enigma whose solution alone now seemed to him above all others necessary, even were he to pay for it the reprehensible price of his own life which was, in any case, inextricably bound up with it.

One cold morning in November, Albert entered the room Herminien had just left. The yellow rays of the sun, streaming through the high windows, greeted him on the threshold, traversed its whole immense length, and seemed gloriously to *devastate* it like the sword of the avenging angel. At first glance it appeared that this large and empty room would hardly offer any of the surprises that Albert, with the naïve and frenzied excitement of a child, might have imagined in advance. But above all, was the soul overwhelmed by an air of savage liberty permeating the whole atmosphere, by the blinding and stark streaming of the light which seemed to bring with it into the room the *air of the high seas* dilating the lungs even to the limit of its own incalculable volume, and the rockets of light that traversed the apartment and that seemed to be supporting it like girders, called to

mind in the most striking manner, the extraordinarily *serene* atmosphere with which Dürer surrounds the
figure of the Evangelist. Entire plains of a buoyant
and translucid air, charged with an exhilarating odour,
were contained between these high walls.

Quickly Albert went over to a heavy oaken bookcase occupying one side of the room, filled entirely
with thick leather volumes which at first glance seemed
to have been until now completely neglected by Herminien. Only in one corner an inextricable conglom-
eration of books, engravings and prints overflowing
onto the floor in heaps, revealed the persistent and
suggestive activity, even in these desolate regions
given over to wind and sun, of this mind whose preoccupations—although secret and not easily fath-
omable—had not escaped Albert altogether. At first
Herminien's reading did not appear particularly significant—and would have struck an ordinary
observer only by the pronounced taste for speculation it at once revealed. Although his tastes had
tended, and evidently with an ever-growing passion,
toward metaphysical research, it was also clear that
certain epochs of human thought had held him by
their persistent charm, and more especially the period
toward the decline of the Alexandrine school of philosophy, as well as the first dawning of what is usually
called German idealism, and which shines with such

sibylline brightness through the glorious works of Schelling and Fichte. But such enticements were too familiar to Albert himself to hold his attention long—and slowly and pensively he began turning over some ancient and precious engravings—carelessly placed on one of the shelves of the bookcase—which seemed to have been the object of a daily preoccupation, and by their unusual disposition attracted the eye in the same indefinable and inadvertent way that, among a thousand other objects, a detective's eye is caught by an indubitable *piece of evidence*.

The most engaging and successful specimens of human art, avid to preserve unalterably the expressions of a face ravaged by violent and abnormal passion, seemed to be vying with each other here, and made of this unique collection a treasure almost without price. And more particularly the figurations of the mystic ardours of *grace* flooding a woman's countenance, and for a brief moment causing secret splendours, as though released from the coarse grain of the skin like a volatile essence, to flow over its surface, seemed to have been assembled here from all over the world through the urge of some intimate predilection whose overwhelming intensity was manifest in the well-known rarity, apparent to Albert at a glance, of certain examples. But Albert felt his reason falter when, by the operation of a relentless analogy, the last notes of the improvisation which Herminien had given vent to in the chapel, and of which these various engravings Albert was now examining seemed but a timid and awkward graphic evaluation, again burst upon his ear in the highest register and with their fullest splendour.

As he was replacing the engravings on the high shelf of the oaken bookcase in order to wipe his forehead, suddenly bathed in sweat, his attention was drawn for the first time by another engraving of minute dimensions which lay on a stand by Herminien's bed, and whose slightly wavy edges seemed to have kept the traces of recent handling, even, as it were, the warmth of the eager fingers which had only a moment ago seized it and put it down again as in an act of perpetual and ecstatic contemplation. It bore witness to a composition extraordinarily different in every way from the other works Albert had examined, and, in the unbelievable minuteness of detail which the artist had lavished upon it and which seemed to bear the very mark of a fathomless love for his art, approached more particularly the style of certain of the most hermetic works of Dürer.

It represented the sufferings of King Amphortas. Standing in the very centre of a temple, gigantic in its proportions and of a heavy, violent and tortured architecture like that to be seen in the works of

Piranesi, and in which the thickness of the vaulted
ceiling and of the walls, through an almost incredible
effort of genius, seemed indicated in the inclination
of the smooth surfaces alone, and rendered forever
prodigious the vertical descent of a dense and brilliant
ray of sunlight into those abysmal depths, Parsifal
was touching the side of the fallen king with the
mystic lance, and on the very threshold of the miracle the faces of the knights, wrapped in their long
robes, were lighted up with a supernatural exaltation. The delicious confusion of Kundry, the grave
joy of Gurnemanz, the artist had painted with perfect simplicity and truth. Incontestably, this was a
marvellous and singular work, a profound and singular work, and no one could deny its convincing and
sovereign perfection.

And yet such a judgment, however much it implied
an unreserved approbation of the artist's technical and
spiritual resources and the immeasurable and rich harmony with which they were here co-ordinated, *could*
not convey all the significance of this work, nor render,
in the least degree, the perturbation awakened in the
soul of the beholder, which seemed to recur inces-
santly from an uncontrollable contradiction. And in
the last analysis this could be ascribed to the *hierarchy*,
in all points unusual, that the composition in the end
forced upon the spectator's attention. For in this

pathetic couple—which the piercing rays of the sun designated as the heart of the composition and between whom the flash of the Lance formed a link far surpassing the miracle—it was apparent that the face of the divine Saviour paled in the presence of the secret wound from which he had drawn the spell and the ardour forever. And, ignoring a sacrilegious equivalence as in the delirium of an infamous inspiration, it was clear that the artist, whose unparalleled hand could not betray him, had taken from the very blood of Amphortas, which spread in a great pool on the flagstones, the glowing matter streaming in the Grail, and that it was from the wound itself that the flames of an inextinguishable fire surged from every side, whose ardour dried the throat like an unquenchable thirst.

And clear, too, that the guileless and faithful knight no longer hoped at the end of his quest, whose painful and uncertain vicissitudes were evident in the dust that dimmed his cuirass, to have found at last the power to close the august revolutions of the Sacred Blood flowing in their fierce mystery in the heart of a universe situated forever outside his reach, but only to consecrate to it the testimony of his life, stamped now forever by the mark of chance with a cruel and provocative gratuitousness. And from the humiliation of the one who had wandered through the world amid untold suffering only to revive forever the radiance of the incomparable wound, and offer the avowal of his henceforth perpetual dependence, one gathered that the artist for his own glorification had obscurely wished to suggest that the quality of saviour was never obtained but always given, and could in no case be measured by merit, but only by the permanence of its inexhaustible effects. For in one corner of the engraving framed in an iron ring hanging on the wall, he had himself paraphrased his work in the bitter device, which seems forever to close—and to close forever around nothing but itself, the *cycle* of the Grail: "Redemption to the Redeemer".

X

DEATH

SOON HERMINIEN'S HEALTH seemed completely restored, and once more he and Albert engaged in those interminable conversations, resumed not from force of habit alone but above all because of the irritating pleasure afforded by the knowledge that between them there now existed a forbidden subject. For Albert—while Heide, whom he saw only at rare intervals and whose life, now completely vegetative and as though consumed by a fanatical love, was spent almost entirely in the twilight of her own room, remained an ever-living presence in his heart—these conversations, although their content remained perfectly insignificant, soon became the object of a daily *anguish* which would strike his heart with a sudden shock whenever in one of the corridors could be heard the reverberation of his friend's nonchalant step. And yet never had their thoughts seemed more vigorously lucid, more unerring and profound their analyses whenever abstruse questions of philosophy, and more particularly of aesthetics, arose between them. But, sometimes, having reached the heart of a complicated discussion, the sound of their mingling voices would seem brusquely suspended, their thoughts would ebb like the waves of the sea suddenly driven back to their profoundest depths, and their glances cross with the silent glitter of steel.

Meanwhile, one by one, the days went by, taking with them the last vestiges of Herminien's illness, and for Albert the now fatal hour of Herminien's departure approached; for he *could no longer* be separated from Herminien, and with all the power of his mind, he hailed, like a flood of refreshing waters, the advent of the denouement in which his own life and death would be at stake, but which would instantly terminate the atrocious tension that had ravaged his whole body ever since his walk through the forest. And the days that fled, ever shorter and shorter, ever darker and darker, lent to Herminien's presence, ever more uncertain, an agonizing and mournful charm, and this black and fraternal angel, this Visitor of the dark cloak who was bathed in such a fatal mystery, and whose departure must remove forever any chance of *knowing*, Albert would now willingly have forced to stay with the irony of cries, tears and the most ardent supplication.

In the course of these familiar and listless conversations, it was soon disclosed that the long days Herminien had spent away from Argol had been employed in researches—extremely precise and meticulous, and which had led him to explore completely forgotten files of the archives of Brittany—on the history of the castle and the circumstances of its construction, which seemed to go back to the remote period of the Norman invasions and the incomparably bloody battles the Bretons, then recently landed in this melancholy country, had waged against the invaders. These discoveries—which included in particular a detailed plan of the original construction—an extremely rare document which he had been permitted to take out of a museum for a brief period—seemed convincing, and on a leaden afternoon of December which promised in advance a day of complete idleness, Herminien, with singular insistence, suggested to Albert that they should verify the existence of a secret passage whose *entrance* alone was clearly indicated by references in the parchment, as though its *destination* must, at all costs, be kept secret, and of which no recollection remained in the memory of the servants, all of them old inmates of the castle, no trace in the numerous legends familiar to all the peasants of this region whose perturbing centre was Argol.

They went down to the great drawing-room which the murky pallor of the sky filled with a dreary dusk, still further darkened by the heavy silken draperies which Albert, going over to the window, for a moment drew aside. Thick clouds rushed across the sky, heralds of a tempest which, from all indications, seemed imminent, and the wind filled the naked woods with a furious, continuous hissing. The atrocious desolation of these boundless spaces suddenly pierced his heart with the chill of steel. Meanwhile Herminien, having taken some mason's tools out of a bag, began to tap the thick walls in the place where the secret aperture was indicated on the plan, and soon both of them, with a strange, absorbed attention, were listening to the blows on the smooth wall, whose echo seemed to reverberate through the most remote corridors of the castle like an awaited dagger blow. For a long time they pursued their search in vain but, suddenly, as Herminien's fingers, feeling for some interstice in the wall, inadvertently pressed the head of a large copper nail that secured the rods holding the long draperies, the startling click of some secret mechanism was heard, and one of the panels decorating one end of the wall, sliding open without effort, revealed a yawning black orifice within. A breath of cold air blew in their faces, and Herminien, seizing one of the copper candelabra standing on a nearby console, beckoned Albert to follow him.

In the hazy and flickering light of the candle Herminien held, it was evident from the dilapidated state of the place thus revealed, that this subterranean passage, accomplice of some secret and criminal love, had from time immemorial been left to slow decay. Great masses of heavy rubble fallen from the narrow vault, lay scattered on the ground, and on every side the flaking walls, betraying throughout the persistent humidity of the climate, appeared to be covered with a whitish efflorescence. The peculiar odour of wood that has for a long time been enclosed in a damp place, assailed their nostrils. Meanwhile, as they made their way with some difficulty through masses of fallen plaster and debris hanging down from the mouldering beams, Albert pointed out, with a feeling of uneasiness, that the long spiderwebs imprisoning the dust of ages in their meshes, and whose unbroken web *should* have stretched across the entire width of the vault, as though torn by some recent passage, *hung* down along the walls, draping them with their sordid folds and leaving in the middle of the vault an inexplicably free space.

The direction of the passage was at every moment changed by sharp turns, so that it was not long before they were completely lost. However, it soon became evident after they had climbed several flights of decayed and crumbling stairs which at intervals blocked the vault, that the exit would be found in one of the upper storeys of the castle. But only an impenetrable silence on Herminien's part greeted this remark proffered by Albert, with a passionate eagerness hardly warranted by the, on the whole, insignificant character of the observation, and whose accent surprised Albert himself. Soon they came face to face with a wall made of rude oaken timbers, and Albert's heart began to beat with an emotion that curiosity alone could not altogether explain, while Herminien's fingers groped in the darkness with meticulous haste, and quickly found the mechanism which controlled this final issue. The heavy oak panel slid back without a sound, and Albert and Herminien found themselves in Heide's chamber. At this late hour of the declining day, an almost total obscurity reigned throughout the room filled with the redolence of a penetrating perfume which floated around the furs and white draperies, while on every object lay the seal of so secret an intimacy that Albert and Herminien hesitated as though on the threshold of some forbidden sanctuary.

The bed, toward which Albert's glance now turned, in the traces of infinitely graceful and voluptuous curves, bore the recent imprint of a woman's body which still seemed to be crushing it with its rich and omnipotent splendour, with the ravishing weight of its weary limbs—and his whole body was seized with a horrible trembling. For a long time they remained silent. Had Albert then turned from the depths of his anguish toward Herminien, he might perhaps have seen flitting across his friend's lips a cunning smile whose indubitable and scabrous *insolence* revealed the consciousness of his imperturbable self-possession, seeming to confirm that singular detachment shown by him, in the course of this exploration, toward all those details which he had observed with the *sang-froid* of a spectator who foresees with complete lucidity the outcome in advance. Little by little total darkness took possession of the room, and the reddish flickerings thrown by the candle now near its end, lighted it as for a vigil to which the prolonged silence added a character of intolerable solemnity. And when once more they entered the subterranean passage, its sordid darkness seemed to bring to both of them a feeling of unexpected *relief*.

For Albert, the evening passed in sombre silence. Vainly he sought oblivion in the cool darkness of his pillows—the nitrous atmosphere, increasing with the approach of the December storm, thick and suffocating, chased away all thought of sleep, and half reclining he remained for a long time listening to the drumming, which seemed startlingly close, of the rain drops on the window-pane, as though indefatigably driven out of the profound night now shaken to its depths by the furious gusts of wind. No, such a night was not meant for sleep! With a hand that shook with fever, he lighted a candle standing on the table by his side, and, suddenly, out of the darkness at the far end of the room, reflected in the high crystal mirror loomed his enigmatic image.

The change that had come over his physiognomy in the course of these last few weeks had now assumed an almost terrifying character, and his strong constitution seemed to be completely undermined by the effects of a disease whose symptoms pointed to none of the ordinary maladies. His dilated nostrils, whose diaphanous membranes gave to his expression such an air of lofty spirituality, now had a waxy consistency that seemed to betray a slow wasting away of the living tissue. A bitter line showed at the corners of his mouth. But above all, his eyes, which burned with a tremulous glow like that of a beacon in their hollow orbits, as though transfigured by the expression of a constant *fear* far surpassing all other horrors, and whose profound ravages attested to its indubitably familiar character now reflected in the depth of that mirroring obscurity, suddenly struck him with such horror and disgust that, seizing the copper candelabrum, with demented fury he hurled it against the glass, which shattered into a thousand pieces and lay scattered over the floor. Then in the inky darkness, like a bubble of poisonous gas, from the depth of his memory rose the recollection of that tortured night, and on the festive, the magnificent bed all adorned in its white draperies, glimpsed for an instant in the flickering candle light, appeared Heide's naked image that he had evoked from the fresh contours of her overwhelming imprint, and beside her like a sombre and unleashed angel, surrendering himself to all the frenzy, all the petrifying bliss of sacrilege, it seemed to him that Herminien with a terrible fixity kept his eyes riveted on the dazzling wound—and suddenly everything around them seemed to vanish—and between him and this atrocious and hypnotic couple the humid gulfs of night seemed suddenly to roll back, tearing open a fathomless and boundless space, and hurling him always farther away, forever cut off, forever alone, forever separated, without any possibility of appeal, of pardon, or redemption, far from what he now knew would *never again* exist. "Never again." Out of his delirium he pronounced the words in a half whisper, and the sound of his voice as though coming from a stranger's mouth—so deeply was he plunged in the absorbing intensity of his vision—suddenly completely roused him.

With a meticulous deliberation, with movements suddenly of a disconcerting precision, strangely in contrast to his recent demented gesture, seeming to indicate a second state similar to that of a sleepwalker, he rose and dressed completely. For a moment he pushed open the sashes of the lofty windows and, leaning on the window bar, clasped in both his

hands his forehead bathed in sweat, and the soul of
Herminien, suddenly fraternal and reconciled, seemed
to come toward him on the breath of the tempest,
and touched his forehead with an icy coldness, with
an appeasement beyond that of death itself. Out of a
chest he took a finely chased dagger and, with a
mad smile, for an instant tried the sharp edge on
one of his fingers; then, closing the window as though
regretfully on the yellow illumination of the storm
now at its height, and with rapid steps, through the
deserted corridors he made his way to the great
drawing-room. With an odd and almost solemn slowness, the secret panel glided back without effort under
his fingers.

Long hours later, out of a heavy and dreamless
slumber, he was aroused by cries reverberating
through the entire mass of the castle, and seeming of
such an alarming and abnormal urgency—waking him
out of a sleep almost as profound as that of drunken-
ness—that he was brought to a half-consciousness of
the significant *lapse of time* that had passed for him outside his room and, his heart suddenly suffocated by a
supreme anguish, he threw his cloak hastily over his
shoulders and hurried to Heide's chamber. Heide was
dying, and the pallor on the faces around her made it
evident that all succour was now in vain. Near her a
vial, still half-full of a dark liquid, showed to what a

potent remedy she had turned in order to flee a life whose last tie, the only one she was willing to recognize as valid, had been broken for her that night, and in a manner so fatal and so unlooked for. And her face, buried in her pillows, and which she had covered with her bloodless hands in a gesture of impotent and childish protection, revealed, even before the slow advent of the longed-for death, in the anguish of a terrible haste, that she had already sought the invincible oblivion of her tortures in the rivers of a *night* without stars and without a tomorrow, which seemed now to be covering her on all sides with a surprising peace and under an immense thickness. And from Albert's eyes and from his throat, in the utterly unexpected horror of this ultimate gesture, that seemed appallingly to bear witness against him before God and man, poured the bitter and fiery tempest of the tears and sobs of damnation. With his hands, with his lips buried in the folds of her robe of innocence, in the midst of demented kisses he endeavoured to warm her cold face and, wildly throwing himself on the bed, in a mournful embrace would have wrested her body, already submissive, subjugated and yielding, even in its most secret molecules and already governed by laws eternally different, from the stern and final suzerainty of death—then uttering a prolonged and savage cry, he fainted.

The preparations for burial were quickly accomplished. The sun hid behind thick mists as Albert and Herminien, carrying Heide's fragile coffin on their shoulders, their wild locks horribly twisted by the last gusts of the tempest, slowly made their way to the graveyard on the shore. Strangely silent was their funereal journey—through an unreal and feathery mist that clung to all the asperities of the ground, muting the sound of their footsteps and the monotonous crackings of the wooden planks so hastily assembled. They came to the far end of the bay and Albert, putting his mouth to Herminien's ear, in a few brief words spoken in a hissing, hollow, and suddenly lifeless voice, reminded him by what an unerring and now particularly sinister coincidence the place of Heide's grave had been long ago *designated*. They once more read the inscription on the stone, and Herminien acquiesced in silence. They dug the grave, they lowered the coffin into its humid bed, then Albert, scooping up a handful of dry sand and leaning over the grave in an attitude of grim meditation, let the warm grains slowly filter through his fingers like a liquid of death, and the delicate bullets could be heard rebounding on the varnished planks with a mournful resonance.

The evening found Albert and Herminien together in the great drawing-room where all the lamps, burning for them alone in a dazzling illumination as for a deathly *celebration*, threw light into the farthest corners of that vast room. And for the first time Herminien brought up the subject of his coming departure, and speaking as of a now irrevocable *decision*, he represented it as determined by the singular circumstances in which death had visited the castle, and particularly by the heavy responsibility which he, Herminien, more than anyone, had indubitably incurred by bringing to these solitary and lugubrious regions a person for whom their relationship, without even taking into account its adventurous and hardly definable character, had certainly always borne the particularly striking mark of (and he oddly insisted on the word) *ill-luck*, constantly confirmed. And although he put forward his reasons in order, and in a matter-of-fact tone that appeared now fiercely ironic, he was not unaware that the air of resignation scarcely tinged with regret, even of *indifference*, with which Albert received them in all their tedious development, concealed without a doubt some secret reticence, difficult to probe and that left a growing uneasiness floating in the air during the rest of the evening which Herminien, nevertheless, seemed anxious to prolong, as though to study a little longer— and with a concentrated passion usually only aroused by a question of life and death—Albert's still, pale face: but behind that white brow, luminous and impassive in the fantastic flickerings of the countless candles, nothing was now legible. At last they separated and sought their chambers in the upper storeys of the castle.

Sleep did not come to Herminien. The moon had hardly begun to flood the sky with all its splendour, when he went to sit at the window on a white stone bench. Marvellous was the forest in its silver sparkling, in its still and slumbrous sweetness. The river seemed strangely near, shining under its luminous meshes of mist. Yes, calm was Argol under its stars, buried in its meshes of mist, and all enfolded in itself, floating through space with its bewitched and translucid air. And yet, that calm night, that sweet night was the night of the *great departure*, for Herminien's eyes could not lie. Before separating in the great drawing-room they had exchanged a solemn promise—and Herminien shuddered at its fabulous majesty.

For a long time he sat thinking of his youth, of all the years he had known Albert, when between them had been woven those *unavowable* bonds whose noose this night was about to strangle them, to unite them. When still only boys—at a time when the most abstruse, the most perplexing problems of theology attracted them with a singular passion—Albert used to call Herminien his *lost soul*.

In the very middle of the long December night, down the deserted stairs, through the deserted rooms where the candles were burnt out, where the candles were overturned, he left the castle in a traveller's attire. Very rapidly (for he hastened through the cold night) his steps turned toward the magic avenue which Albert and Heide had followed on a fatal day. The folds of his cloak flapped around him like wings, and behind him and in his brain, in those regions of the brain where the exacerbated senses hold sway, footsteps echoed deep in the icy night—his footsteps? Out of the night they came toward him—and, as though he had always expected them, he recognized them. But he did not look back toward the mysterious traveller. He did not look back. Quickly he started to run down the middle of the avenue, and the footsteps *followed*. And out of breath now, he felt that they were about to overtake him and, in the omnipotent weakness of his soul, he felt the icy flash of a dagger gliding between his shoulder blades like a handful of snow.